A single shot from a sniper rifle echoed through the camp

Sergeant Mack Bolan sat up and peered over a short wall of sandbags, using the scope of his weapon to scan the tree line. The only movement came from a squad that had been out manning the LPs. The sniper had fled.

Bolan slung his rifle and walked up the hill toward where he'd left Corporal Martin, but he rushed forward when a flurry of activity caught his eye.

Blood stained the hands and clothes of the men kneeling beside the body on the ground.

"Jack!" Bolan yelled. The bullet had caught Martin in the throat. He was slumped on his side, blood covering his face. The Executioner didn't need a medic to tell him that his friend was dead.

Without a word, Bolan returned to his tent, stripped off his T-shirt and got into his gear. He'd had enough. The VC sniper known as the Rifleman had made his last audacious move, killed his last American. The Executioner was going hunting.

MACK BOLAN®

The Executioner

DON PENDLETON's EXECUTIONER

MACK BOLAN.

Warrior's Revenge

A GOLD EAGLE BOOK FROM
WORLDWIDE.

TORONTO • NEW YORK • LONDON • PARIS
AMSTERDAM • STOCKHOLM • HAMBURG
ATHENS • MILAN • TOKYO • SYDNEY

First edition October 1988

ISBN 0-373-61118-8

Special thanks and acknowledgment to
Kevin Randle for his contribution to this work.

Theirs not to make reply,
Theirs not to reason why,
Theirs but to do and die.

—Alfred, Lord Tennyson
"The Charge of the Light Brigade"

It is a high thing, a bright honor, for a man to do
battle with the enemy for the sake of his children,
and for his land . . . and death is a thing that will
come when the spinning Destinies make it come.

—Grecian lyric

Some say a warrior makes his own luck on the
battlefield, and I can't argue with that. But when
mine runs out, I'll stare Death in the face—and
know that the path I chose was right.

—Mack Bolan

To the American soldier

PROLOGUE

Baking in the late afternoon sun, the Camp of the People's Victory sat in the center of a rice field in what had once been Three Corps. The prisoners, burned a deep brown by their years of captivity, toiled in the paddies outside the barbed wire fences and mud walls, growing food that would be sold in Ho Chi Minh City. They were skinny, sweating men whose lives existed at the whim of their captors, men who had lost all hope and faith and waited for death because that was the only release they could expect. They kept their heads bowed, working in the knee-deep, foul-smelling water, ignoring the activities of the guards around them, ignoring the sounds from the highway to the south and the airplanes overhead.

Colonel Dang Van Diem stood on the porch of his hootch, a hand to his eyes to shade them from the blazing sun, and watched the men in the fields. There were guard towers at the corners of his camp where men armed with machine guns passed the night. During the day, the guards, armed with AK-47s or M-16s and even a few of the newer AK-74s, followed the prisoners into the fields to prevent them from trying to escape.

Diem raised his hand and removed the khaki-colored pith helmet from his head, wiping at the sweat and blinking in the bright sun as he watched the men working the paddies. The scene was something that could be replayed all over Vietnam, except that the men were bigger than the Vietnamese and their skin was lighter. These were men who had come from distant lands to fight the Vietnamese and who had lost in that fight. Now they were prisoners, held in case the enemy of that long-ago war decided to come back to fight again. These men were being held as bargaining chips in case bargaining was necessary. They were Hanoi's ace in the hole.

Diem put his hat on and turned, stepping into the hootch that was his office, his headquarters and his home. It was a small wooden structure with two rooms. The front was the office and was furnished with a wooden desk, two chairs, a bookcase and a large portrait of Ho Chi Minh. The back room contained his cot, a night table and his spare uniforms. Not much to show for twenty-two years of military service.

He sat down at his desk, uninterested in the paperwork stacked there: reports from other camps, instructions for educating the prisoners and requests for information about them. It was too hot and muggy for him to work. The ceiling fan was broken and the camp generator had failed again. The one man who could fix it was in the fields planting rice with the rest of the prisoners, and Diem didn't want him to know how valuable his talent was. He'd rather suffer through the heat of the afternoon than admit that none of the Vietnamese understood the generator.

It hadn't always been like this. Once he had been a warrior like those revered in the stories told by the political officers who came to the camp. Once he had been a soldier who hunted in South Vietnam, killing the enemies who had invaded his land. He had been the subject of the stories told by the political officers in the camp rallies then.

Those had been good days. Long, frightening days, but good ones nonetheless. There had been challenge and excitement, and the people had respected him. But not now. He was nothing more than a jailer, and the people didn't respect him. It took no courage, no special ability to hold the white men in their prison.

He remembered working his way through the jungle outside a huge base, walking through the thick vegetation as though he were strolling through a park in central Hanoi. Birds swirled about overhead, monkeys screamed in the trees, rattling the leaves as they jumped from branch to vine and hundreds of insects buzzed incessantly. There was the constant noise of the Americans at work—jets and helicopters crisscrossing the sky, artillery firing and exploding, huge yellow machines clawing at the jungle, pushing it away from the fragile wires they erected to protect themselves.

As Diem approached the edge of the jungle, he slowed his movement, finally dropping onto his belly so that he could crawl forward. He held his rifle in his hands, using his elbows, knees and feet. It was a slow, sometimes painful process, but a necessary one.

Upon reaching the edge of the jungle, Diem halted, his eyes roaming over the open ground in front of him. The bushes, trees and elephant grass had been bulldozed and then burned to eliminate the concealment for an attacking enemy. The flat ground angled upward slightly for three or four hundred meters. There were six strands of concertina and barbed wire, filled with booby traps, trip flares and claymore mines that skilled sappers could navigate in a matter of minutes, but the Americans felt safe behind their flimsy barricades.

He used the scope on his M1891/30 Mosin-Nagant sniper rifle to survey the enemy base camp. He could easily see the Americans, many of whom were stripped to the waist, working to stack sandbags and unload equipment. There was a great deal of activity at the edge of the camp, where the men would be easy targets, if Diem had deemed them worthy of his special attention.

Instead he searched for an officer, someone with power and position whose death would mean something to the brass who ran the war, a death that would strike a little terror into the hearts of all the men at the camp because even the officers couldn't be protected.

The sniper settled in slowly, dragging a rotting log closer to use as a rest for his weapon. He glanced right and left but saw nothing to indicate that the enemy was patrolling near him. The shot, if he chose to make one, would be just over six hundred meters, nothing too great for an expert with a scoped rifle. He had made some shots, at special targets, at just under a thousand meters and had tried one from fifteen hundred. The bullet had struck the target in the shoulder, knocking him off his feet but not killing him.

He watched the Americans work. He could see their faces clearly through the four-power PE scope—white and black faces, covered with sweat, white and black men working hard together in the hot sun.

The officer approached late in the day, arriving in a jeep driven by a sergeant. Both the officer and the noncom leaped out and walked over to inspect the working men. Diem tracked him with the sight post, waiting for the right moment to pull the trigger. There would be time for only one shot. If he took two, the enemy would probably spot him and kill him.

Diem kept the scope on the officer. He was a tall, slender man in starched fatigues who wore a helmet with a camouflaged cover that had a black eagle sewn on. The sleeves of his flak jacket and jungle fatigues were rolled halfway between the elbow and the shoulder. His pistol belt held a small first-aid kit, a pouch for his sunglasses and a holster. The man walked with self-importance, pointing at his subordinates and shouting orders.

One of the workers approached and snapped off a perfect salute. Diem grinned because that identified the man as being important. He knew that most American officers didn't like being saluted in the fields, and that it was only the highest ranking who demanded the courtesy.

Diem put the sight post on the chest of the officer and held there. His 7.62 mm round, even at six hundred meters, should have the power to punch through the flak jacket, which was designed to stop shrapnel but not bullets.

The sniper tried to relax. He took a deep breath, exhaled and took another. As the sight post aligned on the target and the American stopped moving to talk to some of the soldiers, Diem exhaled partway. He steadied his aim and began to squeeze the trigger, letting the weapon fire itself.

Through the scope, Diem saw the round strike, a bloodless third eye appearing in the center of the man's forehead, just below the rim of his helmet. The officer went down bonelessly, and those around him dived for cover. Random shots were fired, one of them passing harmlessly over Diem's head. He grinned at that because he knew that no one on the camp had seen the muzzle-flash or spotted his hiding place.

Until dark he watched the Americans scramble. First they had dragged the dead officer under cover, and then waited while an ambulance rushed up. The green boxy vehicle had huge white squares with red crosses painted on the sides, making it a perfect target for other Vietcong gunners—if there had been any around to shoot at it.

Mortars were randomly fired into the trees around the camp in an attempt to kill the sniper, but none fell near Diem, and it wasn't until dusk that the first enemy patrol began to work its way out of the camp. The twelve men didn't try to conceal their movements, but were noisy and easily tracked. It was nothing for him to worry about.

When it was completely dark, Diem moved. First he drank from his canteen and ate a handful of rice. Nourished, he began the slow task of crawling to the rear, away from the edge of the jungle and the American camp, moving in complete silence so that he didn't give the enemy patrol any clues to his location. Around him were the natural sounds of the jungle, the night sounds—animals prowling, insects buzzing and a light breeze rattling the bushes and trees, covering the little noise that he made.

Now, years later, sitting in his office, Diem grinned once again. That had been a good mission. One bullet, one shot and one dead American. It was what being a soldier was all about. It was not about watching over old men who no longer had the will to live.

The door opened and one of his guards entered. The man stopped in front of the desk. "Comrade Colonel, we have had some trouble."

Diem immediately assumed that one of his prisoners had suddenly developed the will to escape and had tried to run from the camp. Perhaps one of the guards had shot the prisoner. But that was not the case.

"One of the workers has fallen and cannot get up," the guard reported. "The others say he is suffering from a heart condition and to force him back to work would be to kill him immediately."

Diem stared at the guard for a moment. He was a young man for whom the horrors of the war were distant memories from childhood—memories of bombs falling on Hanoi, but not memories of the sacrifices of the soldiers in the field in the South. He was too young to have experienced the war firsthand. He did not understand that the enemy deserved no quarter and that if the prisoner could no longer work, he was of no use.

The guard stared back for a moment and then lowered his eyes. "They say he needs rest and better food."

"This is not a resort," Diem reminded him.

"No, Comrade, it is not." He looked as if he wanted to say more.

"A worker who cannot work is of no value to us. He is a drain on our limited resources, and it is only our kindness that has permitted him to survive for so long."

"Yes, Comrade. What should I do with the man?"

"Kill him."

1

From nearly a mile away Thomas Ryan watched the prisoners working in the hot sun. He'd been lying in the copse of palm and date trees since early morning, away from the paths used by the farmers to walk to their fields. Slowly he studied the fields around him.

Farmers, dressed in black pajamas and wearing conical coolie hats, were heading out into the paddies. Many of them carried tools. A few walked behind water buffalo. Others, their pants rolled above the knee, worked in the dirty water, tending the young plants.

Ryan set his binoculars down and rocked to the right where he'd put his canteen earlier. He picked it up and drank a small amount of the tepid water, then set it down, lifted his binoculars and turned his attention to the camp.

The guard towers, only four or five meters high, had rusting tin roofs and thatched walls. One contained a searchlight, which no one had manned the night before. The compound was surrounded by a wire-and-mud wall that looked flimsy and easily defeated.

As the sun climbed higher, Ryan saw movement inside the camp—guards, obviously by their uniforms and the weapons they carried. Ryan didn't care about the design of the camp or the number of guards. His mission was strictly observation.

He closed his eyes for a moment and thought that the mission hadn't been too difficult other than the hike across Cambodia. He'd been hard-pressed to keep clear of the many guerrilla bands that roved the countryside.

He'd crossed into Vietnam and hadn't found much to be surprised about there. The highways were still full of traffic, the same kind that had been traveling the roads during the war—military vehicles, many of them Dodges and Fords, and a number of ZILs, Lambrettas, Hondas and bicycles.

And, of course, the people. Ryan had kept away from the highways, watching them from a distance, looking for signs that the Communists were ruling with the iron fist that everyone had expected. Except that it was now more than ten years since the fall of Saigon and those who had opposed the Communists were either dead or in reeducation camps, or had escaped.

Ryan put these thoughts out of his head and returned his attention to the prison camp. He scanned the hootches, looking for a sign of the prisoners supposedly held there. Smoke curled from one area where the cooking fire had been lit. Even after all these years, **the Vietnamese still cooked over open fires.**

As he watched the activity in the camp, he felt the sweat blossom on his forehead and drip down his sides. The air was heavy now, oppressive with the heat of the day. The smoke from the fire hung in the air because there was no breeze to blow it away.

He swept the binoculars over the scene again: the farmers in their fields, the water buffalo and the hootches, some with cooking fires in front of them tended by the women who didn't go into the fields. And then back to the camp.

As he watched, the guards slipped into a military formation, spreading out on the dirty square of land that might have been the parade ground. There was a searing note from a bugle and the men in the hootches began to filter into the yard.

Ryan felt his stomach turn over and his head spin. It was just as everyone had said, just as those initial grainy photos had claimed. The reports were true. The Vietnamese were still holding men hostage.

He shifted around and dug into his pack to retrieve the 35 mm Nikon camera buried there. With the tele-photo lens attached, he could see almost as much as he could through the binoculars. As the men lined up for a head count, Ryan began shooting pictures of them as fast as he could advance the film. Each frame caught the faces of the captives and the captors.

The commandant of the camp appeared, dressed in an immaculate uniform with boots that glowed black. He carried a swagger stick like the ones the Japanese had used in the Second World War. On impulse Ryan snapped his picture.

With the mission suddenly completed, Ryan stuffed the camera back into his rucksack. He lifted the bin-oculars again and studied the white men, looking for a face he recognized. Before he had left Washington he had spent days going through the books that listed the names and ranks of every American MIA in Southeast Asia. In each case there was a photograph, and Ryan had tried to memorize the faces of the twenty-five hundred men still missing. It had been a long, hard task, and the men he was looking at would be twelve or fifteen years older than they appeared in the pictures. Hard years that would take a physical toll that would make it hard to recognize them.

But even with allowing for that he recognized no one. The men in front of him seemed to be older than the American pilots and others would be—men in their sixties and maybe seventies; sick, stooped men who looked as if they were all close to death. Even with the rigors of life in a prison camp, the men looked much older than they should have been.

The formation broke up and the men were herded toward the hootch where the cooking fire burned. They stood in line and filed into the hootch, disappearing for thirty minutes. Then, their breakfast eaten, they were led out into the fields surrounding the camp to begin their work.

Ryan had seen all that he needed to see. He had photographic proof that Congress would have to accept. And just because *he* didn't recognize the men didn't mean someone in the States—at the DIA, the CIA or the other intelligence agencies—wouldn't be able to put names to the faces.

He slipped to the rear, no longer needing to watch the camp. He could hide in the depth of the copse, rest through the heat of the day protected from the sun by the thick leaves of the trees and be on the move after dark. He could get out and take his information to the States and find his story on the front page of every newspaper within hours of his return. Everyone would want to talk to him.

He was still congratulating himself when he heard the bolt of a rifle slam home. His nostrils filled with the smell of gun oil, and a shadow fell across the ground in front of him. Out of the corner of his eye he could see the barrel of an AK-47—or what he thought to be an AK—pointed at his temple. He had let his guard down too much.

For a moment he froze, not sure of what to do. Slowly he eased his hands out in front of him and opened them to show he held nothing. When the rifle barrel retreated, Ryan put his hands on the ground and slowly, cautiously, climbed to his feet, keeping his eyes focused on the jungle floor. Once he was standing, he turned toward the man with the rifle.

He wasn't surprised by the man who stood there. A short, dark man who had a robust body unlike the majority of the Vietnamese, he wore a khaki uniform with blue shoulder boards bordered in red. There was a single stripe on it, but Ryan wasn't sure what that meant.

They stood staring at each other without moving or speaking. The American broke the silence finally by saying, "Is there a problem?"

The Vietnamese pointed at the pistol strapped to Ryan's hip. Slowly he removed the weapon and dropped it onto the ground. As he did so, the man gestured with his rifle at Ryan's gear, as if he wanted him to pick it up.

Ryan reached down and grabbed his rucksack, surprised that the Vietnamese didn't search it first. He shouldered it, buckled the straps and stood there waiting.

The Vietnamese moved to the rear and shoved the barrel of his weapon against Ryan's head. Holding it there with one hand, the man searched the rucksack, tossing a few things onto the ground, out of the way. He then pushed the American away from that spot and stooped to pick up everything, including the pistol he had seemed to ignore.

Ryan turned to face the soldier, suddenly aware of how hot and humid the jungle had become. He was afraid of the man because there was no reason for the Vietnamese to keep him alive. No one knew he had been found, and a well-placed bullet would provide the Vietnamese with everything Ryan owned, not to mention a fresh corpse to exploit. Suddenly he wished he had tried to take the soldier when he had appeared. Kill him quickly, rather than letting the man get the drop on him.

"I am an—" he started to say, then stopped. He wasn't sure identifying himself as an American was the smartest thing he could do. He dropped his eyes and considered his options. After all, he was in the country illegally, armed illegally and spying on the prisoner camp. It would be difficult to talk his way out of this one.

The Vietnamese was examining the camera, turning it over in one hand as if he had never seen anything like it. The barrel of his weapon dropped, pointing toward the ground.

Ryan knew he would never get another chance. He kicked out once, the side of his foot connecting with the barrel, shoving it aside. As that happened, he danced closer, striking with his fist. The blow caught the enemy on the jaw and the man fell. He rolled once and sprang to his feet, swinging his weapon toward Ryan.

The American leaped, landing on the man and shoving the weapon away. He punched at the guy's face, pain flaring through his hand as the jab connected. It rocketed up his arm, but Ryan kept pounding at his adversary.

The soldier bucked, trying to throw him, and slammed his fist into Ryan's shoulder. He lashed out with his feet, trying to knock him off balance, struggling all the while to bring the rifle around and fire.

But the American held him firm, grunting with the effort. He hammered at the man and could feel the delicate bones of the face shatter. The Vietnamese moaned in pain.

In desperation the man twisted around so that he was on his side and grabbed his rifle in both hands, swinging it like a baseball bat. It struck Ryan on the point of the shoulder and his arm went suddenly dead. The nerves sang in pain, and Ryan saw spots swirling in front of his eyes. He slipped to the side.

As the big man fell, the soldier rolled in the opposite direction, suddenly free. He snapped the rifle around and aimed, then pulled the trigger.

The first round caught the American in the shoulder, slamming him backward. White-hot pain flashed through his body, but Ryan ignored it. He twisted to the right and grabbed at the pistol lying in the dirt.

The second shot hit him in the hip, and Ryan was convinced he could feel the bullet strike the bone and fragment. There was a spreading warmness across his crotch that was his blood. He rolled painfully onto his back and fired in return, jerking at the trigger.

Ryan's first shot hit the Vietnamese in the forehead and exploded into his brain, shattering an exit through the rear of the skull and blowing blood and gray matter into the jungle vegetation. The man flipped back, his feet drumming on the ground and his arms flailing around in the air as if fighting off an attack of bats.

Ryan kept shooting until the pistol was empty and the bolt locked back. Then, with great effort, he sat up. His hip felt as if it had been salted with broken glass, and his left arm was useless. He was light-headed and knew that if he didn't stop the bleeding he would die quickly.

He glanced at the wound in his hip—a small entrance hole and no exit. The bullet was lodged in his body, but the bleeding was minimal. It might be impossible to walk, but the wound wouldn't prove immediately fatal.

Ryan shrugged his way free of his rucksack. An inch at a time, he dragged it around so that he could paw through its contents. He tossed his equipment aside until he located the first-aid kit.

Retrieving a pressure bandage, he struggled with one hand to tie it around his shoulder. After he had secured it in place, he was exhausted. He couldn't tell if he had stopped the bleeding or not and then wasn't sure that it mattered. He would never be able to get out of Vietnam on his own. The help he needed was in Tay Ninh City, nearly forty miles away. And he couldn't get there because he knew he wouldn't be able to walk.

He fell back, lying flat on the ground and staring at the sky. All around him he could hear sounds: birds and monkeys, and lizards that scrambled through the vegetation; a distant shout from a farmer, and the bellowing of a water buffalo; insects buzzing and flies swooping in on the open wounds of the dead Vietnamese.

Ryan must have slept. He wasn't sure, but it seemed that time had passed. His clothes were sweat-soaked, and his wounds throbbed with the beating of his heart. The pain was almost too much to bear, and he wanted to scream with it.

The sounds of people coming toward him filled Ryan with relief because he had realized that he would never be able to stand up without help. He would never walk out of there alone. He twisted his head around, trying to see who was approaching.

The men surrounded him just outside his range of vision. They spoke excitedly to one another until a single voice cut through the sound, silencing them. That one man stepped into his field of view. He blotted out the sun so that it looked as if there were a halo around his head. No features were visible, but it was obvious that the man was in uniform.

"Who are you?" Ryan croaked. His voice sounded rusty, and he wished he could get a drink of water.

The man stood there, hands on his hips, shaking his head. "You will soon die, American." His English was heavily accented, sounding as if he hadn't spoken it in a long time.

"Help me," Ryan said. "Please."

The man crouched, resting an elbow on his knee. "What are you doing here?"

Ryan wanted to shrug but couldn't move his shoulders. "I..." he started and then couldn't finish. The elaborate cover story had slipped from his mind. He couldn't think of it as the pain blurred his brain and numbed him. "I was..." he began again and then stopped.

The Vietnamese man reached out and grabbed the front of Ryan's shirt. "Why are you here?"

Ryan wanted to answer but couldn't find the words. He wanted to ask for help but couldn't speak. Instead he closed his eyes and waited.

The man rattled off something in Vietnamese, and Ryan felt hands lifting him and placing him onto a stretcher. He relaxed then, assuming that they would help him. The American embassy in Thailand would be upset with him, and he might be looking at time in jail, but it was better than slowly dying in the jungles of what had once been South Vietnam.

DAVID LEE MCDONALD SAT in his tiny third-floor office in the American embassy in Bangkok and wondered what had gone wrong. He had just returned from the radio room where he had expected to learn that Thomas Ryan had checked in, finally, but that was not the case. He had waited while the radioman tried to initiate the emergency procedures, but there had been no response to that, either. McDonald could only conclude that something had happened to his agent.

Now, sitting behind the battleship-gray metal desk in a chair that squeaked each time he moved, there was only one thing he could do. He turned and used his heels to drag his wheeled chair toward the two-drawer safe and filing cabinet. The air conditioner hummed, blowing frigid air into the small room as he spun the combination dial.

Pulling open the drawer, he thumbed through the files, which weren't arranged according to any of the several sample file plans the government had provided. McDonald found the folder he wanted and yanked it free, shoved the drawer shut and dragged himself back to the desk. He clicked the switch at the base of his desk lamp, throwing a pool of light on the center of his desk.

The emergency procedure was quite clear. Since Ryan had failed to make two scheduled check-in reports, McDonald was required to inform Langley. Then it became their problem. The form for the message, the priority that it was to be given and the addressees were all spelled out for him.

McDonald rocked back and laced his fingers behind his head. He stared at the light green walls that were devoid of decoration except for a single watercolor painted by a local artist. The painting depicted a blonde—wearing only the bottoms of a tiny bikini—standing on a sandy beach, her arms lifted as if to accentuate her naked breasts. McDonald had bought it because the woman looked like someone he had once known.

The last thing he wanted to do was alert Langley to the problem at hand. Although he had become merely the control after Langley had taken over, he had recruited the agent and provided some assistance in equipping him. He hadn't arranged for the local contacts in Thailand, Cambodia or Vietnam, but he would be held responsible. The man had been run through his office, and Ryan's failure became his failure.

He thought about waiting for the next scheduled report, hoping that Ryan would surface, but he was afraid to do that. If Ryan failed to report, then the delay in his forwarding the information would also be noted. That would mean one more black mark on his record.

Of course if he reported Ryan missing and the man called during the next scheduled check-in, McDonald would be criticized for jumping the gun. Sweat broke out on his face, and he touched his forehead to the sleeve of his white shirt.

Finally, when he knew he could wait no longer, he opened the middle drawer of his desk and took out a pen and a legal pad. McDonald wrote out the message suggesting that Ryan was overdue. He had to return to the safe once to get his codebook so that the Soviets, if they intercepted the message, wouldn't be able to read it easily. It would take them a while to understand it, provided they had cracked the new code.

When the message was drafted, he put his codebook and files back into the safe and locked it. Then he stood, moved to the door and exited, locking the door behind him.

He took the elevator down to the message center and rang the bell on the vaultlike door. The peephole opened and a brown eye appeared. A moment later the door swung open and McDonald entered a large, well-lit room in the basement of the embassy where the climate and the access could be controlled more easily. From the back came the clatter of Teletype machines and high-speed printers. There was a buzz and crackle from the radios, and a low murmur as men and women received and answered the transmissions. Most sat at large desks that had several types of radios built into them.

A woman stood in front of McDonald with her hand out. She was a small woman with cropped hair who wore a light dress and a sweater against the chill of the air-conditioning.

"Whatcha got, David Lee?"

"Priority message for Langley." He shrugged helplessly. "I guess the sooner it goes out, the better."

She took the form, initialed it and handed the copy back to McDonald. "Twenty minutes at the most," she said. "Military attaché had a few things he needed to send to the Pentagon."

McDonald was immediately interested. "Anything I should know about?"

"Now, David Lee, you know better than that. If Colonel Clayton wanted you to know, or if he thought you should know, he would copy you on the messages."

"Yes, Jean, but you can tell me if it's anything I should know."

She dropped her voice conspiratorially. "Well, I wouldn't sit on my hands if I were you. I'd go ask the colonel about it."

"Thanks, Jean. I owe you a dinner for that."

"That's what you always say, but you never deliver on the promise. One of these days I'm going to stop believing you'll ever buy that dinner."

"Thanks again." He headed back to his office, wondering what Clayton had learned about Ryan's mission. Had the Army officer heard something that hadn't been passed through normal channels? McDonald would have to find out quickly before the Pentagon people called Langley to gloat. That would really drive a nail into his career coffin.

"You know it's not the sort of thing I do, Hal. Besides, a thousand other men could pull it off."

"Let's ignore that for a moment," Hal Brognola replied. "Won't you at least look at the information?"

Mack Bolan closed his eyes, fatigued. The last thing he needed was another trip to Southeast Asia when there were so many pressing matters here at home.

Brognola continued, "You're a Vietnam veteran yourself. I know that you have empathy for these men who are labeled as missing in action."

"Empathy, yes—if there's evidence that they're being held. But there are avenues to be pursued that have nothing to do with me. You're looking for a jungle adventurer to go in to find proof. If I go in, I bring people out."

Brognola took a deep breath. "I understand what you're saying, Striker, but we can't bring the men out yet. Politically that wouldn't help the situation. It could force the Vietnamese to eliminate other soldiers being held."

"It's beginning to sound like you already have the answers."

"Let me show you the briefing package." He held up a hand to stave off any protest. "You won't be obligated in any way. It'll just show you what we have and tell you what we need."

Like most Americans, Bolan was enraged by the thought that American soldiers and sailors might be held in Vietnam as some kind of living bargaining chip, but there had never been any tangible proof of it. Stories told by escaping Vietnamese and mercenaries in Vietnam were unreliable, at best, and the few photographs that had been presented lacked detail. It was difficult for Bolan to believe that the American government would overlook the evidence if it was there.

Brognola confirmed that by saying, "We don't have anything concrete, but we do have indications of a couple of prison camps, one of them in the Saigon-Tay Ninh vicinity. Here, let me show you."

The big Fed opened his briefcase and set a file folder on the desk. He extracted a map from the file and spread it open. "The reports we have state that the camp lies here, around the old American base at Cu Chi. Not on the site of that camp, but close to it."

Bolan glanced at it and nodded. "Okay. If you know that much, why don't you put someone in to check it out?"

"That's what I'm trying to arrange," Brognola answered dryly.

The warrior sat back in the chair and stared at his old friend, but said nothing.

"We have a few pictures that fell into CIA hands." He spread them out on his desk as if they were a new deck of cards.

Again Bolan leaned forward, picking up the first photo and examining it. He could tell by the graininess that it had been taken from a long distance with a telephoto lens. Some detail of the camp's walls and wires were visible. A few men—Vietnamese—stood guarding taller, thinner men. Bolan dropped the photograph back onto the desk and picked up the next one.

Brognola sat back and tented his fingers under his chin. "There's no official support for this mission. If anything happens, the United States will disavow all knowledge—a private citizen working without the sanctions of the federal government financed in the private sector."

As Brognola talked, Bolan looked at the remaining pictures. It was idle curiosity more than anything else. Granted, he did help out the big Fed from time to time, but he was free and clear to refuse a mission. He'd recently returned from Vietnam, and he wasn't in a hurry to go back. Had he been the only man who could do the job, well, that would have been different. But he wasn't. Any Special Forces soldier could handle the job. It required a jungle fighter's skill, knowledge of the dangerous flora and fauna and a self-reliance for survival. All Special Forces soldiers had those abilities.

And then he came to the last photo, which showed the camp commander standing on the porch of his hootch, talking to several of his subordinates. Bolan felt his guts twist. His fingers tightened on the picture, and suddenly he was across the Big Pond in a steaming, sticking jungle, hidden from view with only his rifle and his gear.

SERGEANT MACK BOLAN LAY in the deep elephant grass on the slight rise and didn't move. Spread out below him was a wide valley with a river running through its centre. A tree line, following the path of the river, marked its course and provided the enemy with concealment. Between the trees and the slight rise were rice paddies, farmers' mud hootches and a single dirt track, which was the only road.

Behind him, three or four hundred meters away, was the jungle, a thick tangled growth that hid the twelve members of the security squad detailed to guard his back—twelve men from a leg outfit who didn't completely understand the jungle but who were fairly good at surviving in it.

Bolan had been in the blind since before dawn, crawling to it under the cover of darkness, taking three hours to travel the relatively short distance. He had lain in the chill morning air, watching the drifting white fog as it had seeped between the trees along the river, making them look as if they were burning. He had felt the warming touch of the morning sun as it had begun its climb, the rays quickly heating his back and baking him relentlessly.

The soldier ignored the discomfort of lying completely still and let the sweat drip from his face and run into the collar of his jungle fatigues. His uniform had long since been soaked. But still he didn't move. Instead he let his eyes roam the ground in front of him, searching for the enemy he knew was out there somewhere.

Slowly he raised his binoculars and studied the tree line seven hundred meters away. The jungle seemed to be devoid of animal life, and there was a quiet to the scene that suggested a more peaceful setting.

The farmers worked their fields, ignoring everything around them. A jet screaming by overhead failed to gain their attention—they were afraid to look up, afraid that looking up would bring unwanted attention to them. Instead, they bowed their heads and worked harder, tiny, skinny men in black shirts and black shorts, some wearing the conical coolie hat that kept the sun off them.

At noon the men in the fields slipped away, returning to their hootches for a meal. Women worked around the smoking fires, cooking the rice and fish heads that would make lunch.

Bolan watched all the activity carefully, searching for a sign of something out of place, someone who didn't belong in the fields below. A young man stumbled from one of the hootches, stretched and then studied the farmers contemptuously. He pushed his way to a cooking fire and held out a hand, demanding something to eat.

It could be a disgruntled teenager, fed up with a farmer's life, but Bolan didn't think so. There was something about the man that suggested he was more than an unhappy youngster.

A second man appeared at the door of the same hootch. He wore black pajamas but looked like an NVA soldier. His hair, cut so short on the sides that his head looked shaved, was the giveaway. But then he reached back and picked up a rifle easily identifiable as a Russian-designed SKS.

That was all Bolan needed. He shifted slowly, putting his binoculars into their case. Rocking to the right, he slipped his rifle, an M1903A4 with an M73B1 telescopic sight, to his shoulder. Drifting smoke from the fire told him which way the wind was blowing and how strong it was.

Bolan set the windage and focused on the cross hairs on the chest of the man who had picked up the SKS. That weapon was no longer visible, but it had done its job. It had identified the young men as the enemy.

With the sights lined up, Bolan waited for the Vietnamese to stop moving. Since the shot was going to be just over eight hundred meters, he needed a target that was fairly stationary.

The enemy took a bowl from one of the women, scooped out a handful of rice and crammed it into his mouth. He shook his head, then walked toward the hootch, but rather than entering, he sat outside, his back against the mud wall.

For a moment he ate the rice, shoveling it into his mouth with his fingers. When he set the bowl aside, Bolan knew the time had come. He took a deep, relaxing breath, exhaled, then took another. Slowly he began to squeeze the trigger.

Through the telescopic sight, Bolan saw the round strike about a second later. The man jerked once as the specially loaded 179-grain slug slammed into his chest, shattering the breastbone and destroying the heart. He slumped to the side as if he'd just fallen asleep, the black pajama shirt concealing the spreading crimson stain.

The second enemy soldier dropped his bowl of rice and raced to his friend.

Bolan fired his second shot, which caught the man in the middle of his back, blowing through him and splattering the mud wall of the hootch with blood and bone. The bowl was thrown into the air as he collapsed, clumps of rice falling into the spreading stain of red seeping from the body.

When the second shot had left the barrel, Bolan rolled instinctively—he didn't know why he did, but the action saved his life. From somewhere to the right came a shot from a Communist sniper.

Bolan whirled, bringing his weapon to bear, and fired at a shadow in the jungle without taking proper aim, certain that he had missed.

There was a sudden crash behind him and then a ripping burst from an M-60 machine gun as the security squad provided suppressing fire. Bits of lead, bark and wood rained onto the ground as the enemy was peppered with 7.62 mm slugs.

Bolan slipped from his blind and crawled to the rear, keeping his head down. As he reached the light brush, he got to his feet and hurried into the protection of the jungle where the security squad waited, laying down the covering fire.

With his binoculars, Bolan scanned the jungle for a sign of the enemy sniper, but nothing betrayed the enemy's position. Half the security squad swept forward under Bolan's watchful eye and the protection of the other Americans. They found the enemy sniper's nest, but no sign of the man. Bolan knew he would see him again in the very near future.

BROGNOLA WATCHED as the Executioner studied the photo in his hand. The big Fed hadn't spoken for nearly a minute, but Bolan didn't seem to be aware of the sudden silence. He dropped the photograph onto the desktop and looked up.

"There are political reasons for this mission," Brognola told him. "We have to move under cover, because if we're wrong, there'll be hell to pay in the world's arenas. Arrangements for air transportation—a ticket to Bangkok—have already been made. Once there you'll be on your own, an American tourist checking out the sights. You'll be responsible for recruiting your own team—if needed—finding your own guides and getting the weapons you deem necessary. Of course this is a recon and not a direct-action mission. There'll be a briefing with a control officer at Bragg rather than here in Washington."

"Why the precautions?" Bolan asked.

"Well, that's our other problem. A man was sent in a few weeks ago to confirm what these photos show, and he disappeared without a word. There could be any number of reasons for that. Hell, he might have stepped on a snake and been fatally bitten."

"But you don't think so."

"It would be too big a coincidence," Brognola admitted. "With nearly half a million men in Southeast Asia at the height of the war, we didn't lose many to snakebites. We didn't have that many disappear off the face of the earth, either."

"Maybe you're jumping the gun."

"I don't think so. I think that we've got a real problem growing there and we've got to deal with it. And I don't believe that it's something that can be handled by just anyone."

Bolan held up a hand. "All right, Hal, you've convinced me. When do I leave?"

DANG VAN DIEM STOOD at the entrance of the hootch that had been turned into a cage and stared at the filthy body of Thomas Ryan. The man's hair was matted, and his face caked with the kind of dirt that blood and sweat couldn't wash away. The skin that wasn't covered by grimy bandages was badly bruised. Ryan huddled in the farthest corner. A chain ran from his left ankle to a ring bolted in the center of the wooden floor. A makeshift cot shoved against one wall was covered with filthy straw. Bamboo, lashed together, formed the bars of the makeshift cage. Thatching was woven among the bars.

"Are you prepared to talk now?" Diem asked. He leaned against the bamboo and used the tip of a bayonet to clean his fingernails.

Ryan didn't look up. He kept his eyes focused on the floor and shook his head slowly. "Nothing more to tell," he croaked through cracked lips.

"Of course there is." The camp commander crouched so that his eyes were level with Ryan's. "Plenty to tell. Who sent you? Why are you here? There is nothing of interest for you here."

When there was no response, Diem waved at two guards who stood behind him, signaling them forward. They entered the hootch and grabbed Ryan under the arms, lifting him to his feet. He wailed in pain, his voice rising and falling like a police siren, then cracking.

The guards threw him at the cot. Ryan took a stumbling step and put out his hands to break his fall, rolling right as he hit, trying to protect the wounded hip. As he struck the hard surface, he howled in pain.

Diem reentered the cage, turning his head so that he could breathe in the fresh air at the door. The confines reeked with the animallike odor of Ryan, a stench brought on by the lack of toilet facilities, from the body odor of a man who hadn't bathed in two weeks and from a man who was now sick with infections from his wounds. The healing process wasn't progressing very well at all.

Steeling himself, Diem stepped across the floor, the heels of his boots echoing on the wooden surface. He stopped and stared down at Ryan. "You do not have to live like this," he said, waving an expansive hand. "Look around you. There are men who spend their days in the sun. They are allowed the privileges of bathing, medical care and decent food."

"Nothing," Ryan grated through clenched teeth. "Nothing that I can tell you."

Diem nodded and one of the guards stepped forward. He kicked Ryan in the knee. The agent roared with pain, jerking from side to side, his hands on his leg.

"Nothing!" he repeated.

"I do not believe you. A clandestine trip into our country is not a sightseeing tour. It is a mission directed at the Socialist Republic of Vietnam. It is something sinister and foul, and we will learn all that we can about it."

Diem sat down on the edge of the cot, like a doctor conferring with a patient. "You must know that we do not want to see you injured further or to see you die, but we must have your cooperation. If it is not forthcoming, then the situation is out of my hands."

"Nothing to tell," Ryan grated.

"Medical treatment for your wounds," Diem offered. "A little information will go a long way. Let us know why you're here, and I'll see about getting you another shot to fight the infection. If not, there is nothing I can do for you."

Ryan remained silent, his eyes on the Vietnamese officer. The pain had subsided slightly, but the fever from the infection blurred his vision. Sweat beaded his forehead and soaked his tattered clothes and bandages.

Diem stood, shrugging. "So be it."

As the colonel reached the door, the two guards moved past him. One of them jerked Ryan from the cot and held him upright while the other struck him with his fist. Diem stopped and watched as the guards achieved a rhythm, hammering at Ryan's face and then his body, not caring whether they broke bones or reopened the wounds. Diem shook his head as if he were helpless in the situation.

When he stepped into the bright afternoon sunshine, the heat washing over him in a soggy, humidity-laden wave, he glanced at the other white men in the fields. Their guards sat in the shade of the trees at the edges of the rice paddies, drinking from the canteens. They ignored the men because they knew they wouldn't try to escape. A sad situation.

From the cage behind him came the quiet moaning of the wounded, sick man. The impact of the fists had stopped for a moment while the guards rested. They would begin again in a few minutes, keeping at it until Ryan lost consciousness. They would beat on Ryan, taking him to the edge, then back off, making the punishment last for hours.

Diem moved quickly across the open ground to his headquarters hootch. He entered and dropped the swagger stick he carried onto his desk. The interrogation was going as planned. While it was true that the American had said nothing, it was obvious that he was an agent of the Central Intelligence Agency sent to spy on the camp. CIA operatives were told that everyone talks eventually, and this prisoner would be no different. When you didn't expect your agents to remain silent, they wouldn't. Diem's job was to separate the cover story from the reality of the situation, which shouldn't be too difficult. It was obvious why the man was there, and it didn't seem likely that anyone could think of a convincing cover story.

He sat behind his desk, then turned to look out into the fields where the men continued to work, doing the same task over and over because there was nothing more important for them to do.

There would be another, Diem knew. The Americans wouldn't stop with the loss of their agent. The CIA would send a second man, and it would be Diem's job to catch him, too.

3

McDonald was worried about Ryan. He'd been missing for quite a while now, and no agents in the area had reported any knowledge of his fate. McDonald was beginning to believe the man was dead. He'd sent messages to headquarters in Langley, suggesting some kind of rescue mission, but each time someone at the other end had advised him to be patient. The problem was being worked on, they kept telling him, but he didn't find that comforting. Ryan's disappearance was beginning to really bother him. He knew Langley would believe that it was somehow his fault.

He thumbed through the message traffic, reading the secret and top-secret reports being filed from around the globe. Each report described in detail some event in the world, from the latest out of Lebanon to what was happening in Central America. The sources were CIA agents in residence in those areas, military officers and embassy personnel. Most of the information would be available in *Time* or *Newsweek* within days. His advantage was that he received it earlier.

He went over the reports from Southeast Asia carefully. He learned that Russian aircraft were landing at bases that had been built by the Americans during the

Vietnam War; China was selling arms to various Third World countries and suppressing the demonstrations in Tibet with violence; the Soviet presence in Afghanistan hadn't been reduced, and there were more reports of chemical warfare against the locals. There were also continuing reports of chemical warfare in Cambodia, too, but there was absolutely nothing from Vietnam that would suggest they had captured an American inside their borders.

But that was exactly what McDonald had expected. First there would have been some indication in the classified diplomatic traffic, an alert that a big announcement was imminent. To McDonald it meant that Ryan was dead, but not captured. If the Vietnamese had him, they would exploit the opportunity. Even if Ryan withheld the information that he was a CIA agent, the Vietnamese would announce to the world that he was. It was a propaganda coup too good to pass up.

McDonald read through his stack of classified reports. Each was rated according to the accuracy of the information, and the declassification instructions were printed on the front of each report. Most wouldn't be downgraded until 2008, long after McDonald had it shredded because he didn't have the file space to safeguard it for twenty years.

When he finished, he locked the reports into his safe, telling himself he would file them properly in the morning. Now all he wanted to do was to get out of there and onto his date with Rachel Jamison, the daughter of a British diplomat who had abandoned her and her mother shortly after Rachel's birth. McDonald didn't mind her unsavory past because he didn't plan to have anything to do with her after his posting was changed. There were no plans to marry the lady. She was just someone with whom he passed the time.

McDonald walked to the door, stopped, looked back to make sure he had closed the safe, then turned off the lights. He locked the office door and hurried down the corridor to the elevator, which he rode to the ground floor. He passed through the lobby, nodding to the secretary who sat behind the ornate reception desk, swept by the Marine guards who protected the embassy grounds and stepped into the humid evening.

He stopped on the steps, and felt sweat bead on his face and body. A shiver ran up his spine, the result of moving from the air-conditioned building into the tropical heat outside. He pulled his handkerchief out of his hip pocket and mopped his face, then started down the steps, listening to the sounds of the traffic beyond the white walls of the embassy grounds.

To one side, hidden by the tropical plants—thick, broad-leaved bushes, rubber trees, bamboo and palms—was a parking lot where the embassy cars were kept. Staff members were discouraged from using the vehicles kept there for the senior officers. The ambassador and his immediate staff had the use of a limousine, but on a date McDonald didn't want a driver watching his every move in the rearview mirror.

He stopped at the white shack where the head of the motor pool worked. The building looked more like a guard shack, but instead of holding armed men it contained a board with keys, a sign-out sheet for cars and a tiny desk. The supervisor was a Thai man hired back when the Americans were trying to reduce the number of people they brought in from the States. The man was a whiz with the cars but refused to learn English. He spoke a pidgin cross between English and Thai.

McDonald got a car from the motor pool, drove out the gate and entered the main stream of Bangkok traffic. Unlike that of Saigon—now Ho Chi Minh City—Bangkok's traffic was filled with cars and motorbikes. There were few human-powered vehicles. The stench of half-burned diesel fuel and gasoline hung in the air, and crowds of people thronged on the sidewalks.

Palms grew along some of the streets, and sculptured gardens broke the clutter of white stucco buildings with deep greens and bright colors. McDonald drove by a number of greenbelts that were sports clubs or parks. People were packed into some of them while others seemed to be deserted.

He drove through the center of the city, making his way down crowded streets lined with endless shops filled with gold chains and carved elephants, bolts of silk and promises of jewels at ridiculously low prices. The buildings housing these riches were four and five stories high and seemed to have open fronts with block-long counters.

He reached the periphery of the city where the homes were crowded onto small lots. Wooden frame houses, some two stories high, lined the streets now. Some were protected by tall trees, and a few had flowering bushes in front, but most were so close to their neighbors that there was no room for shrubs, gardens or lawns. Patches of dirt separated the houses.

The air almost vibrated with the stench of unwashed bodies and open sewers. Many people sat outside, trying to escape the heat of the tropical afternoon. Children and dogs ran wild, shrieking and barking at one another.

McDonald stopped his car and let the engine idle for a moment as he sat in the air-conditioning, steeling himself for the environment outside. A crowd began to gather, mostly children who stood three or four deep in a circle around him. As soon as he shut off the engine and opened the door, they surged forward, demanding money, candy and cigarettes.

McDonald slammed the car door, grinned at the children and shook his head. They gave up immediately and melted away. He walked to the door of the house and knocked. Rachel Jamison answered his summons.

She was a beautiful woman in whom the Asian and European traits had been mixed to perfection. She had inherited everything that was good from her parents and seemed to have missed that which was bad. Her long, black, silky hair was Asian, but her face was more angular than most Orientals'. Though her eyes were almond-shaped, they were a deep shade of blue instead of brown. She was a tall woman, slender, with a generous bust. McDonald had a hard time keeping his gaze off her chest.

She wore Western-style clothing but seemed to have gotten stuck in the 1960s. Her miniskirt accented her perfect legs and her see-through blouse showed breasts that were held erect by wispy bits of lace and silk.

Jamison reached out, took his hand and dragged him into the house. She glanced right and left, and when she was sure no one was watching, she molded herself to him and kissed him. Her hips rubbed his body slowly, and her tongue probed his mouth. He could smell the delicate scent of her and felt himself responding. She felt it, too, and pressed herself even closer. He let one hand slip from her back to her bottom, cupping it, kneading it gently. From the rear of the house he could hear the quiet conversation of others and music from a local Thai radio station.

Rachel broke the kiss as McDonald decided to see if he could get his hand into her blouse. She grinned at him and shifted her eyes to the corner, warning him that her mother was in the back and they had already violated a number of taboos.

She shouted something in Thai and was answered from someone at the rear of the house. Then they left, walking slowly to the car, bumping into each other. McDonald opened the door and watched as she got in. She made no attempt at modesty. Instead she gave McDonald a glimpse of her thigh and red panties. Once in the car, with the door shut, she made no effort to pull her skirt down, but let it ride up, showing the smooth expanse of her legs.

McDonald got into the driver's seat and put the key into the ignition. He glanced at her again, letting his eyes rest on the perfection of her thighs. He had an almost uncontrollable urge to reach over and slide his hand along the soft inner skin until he could touch the fabric of her panties.

Knowing exactly what she was doing, she scratched her thigh as if it itched, slowly drawing her fingers higher, her nails whispering against her skin.

"Dinner," McDonald said, choking out the word as though there were something stuck in his throat.

"Must we?" she asked, teasing him.

"Well, no, not really. We could drive to my house and see what happens there."

She shifted around so that she was facing him, one leg on the car seat. "But that would not be right. We must have dinner first."

"Of course," he replied, reaching down to pat her on the leg. He tried to slip his hand higher, but she caught his wrist.

"That's for later," she warned him.

"Of course," he repeated and then started the engine.

BOLAN DIDN'T SEE THE NEED for a briefing at Fort Bragg. It seemed ridiculous to him, and he wasn't sure he wanted to visit the base again. It had been part of a previous existence, belonged in another era, another place. Now he was on a small plane that was about to land at the civilian airport.

The flight attendant made a final trip down the narrow aisle, glancing at both sides to make sure everyone's seat belt was fastened. Then she hurried back to the front, sat down in a jump seat facing the passengers and buckled her belt just as the servo whine from the fuselage indicated that the landing gear was being lowered. A moment later there was a bump, then a second, and a roar from the engines as the props were reversed to slow the plane.

When they rolled to a stop and the door was opened, Bolan stood up and followed the other twelve passengers out the door. He stepped from the artificial, recycled air of the aircraft cabin into the heat and humidity of North Carolina. There were no jetways for the commuter plane, just a roped area that led into the terminal.

As he entered the building, a tall man wearing a Class A uniform and carrying a green beret in his hand left the waiting crowds. "You Bolan?"

"Yeah."

"Sergeant Warringer. I have transport arranged. I'll take you over to Fort Bragg."

"Thank you, Sergeant." The Executioner examined the man. The ribbons above his left breast pocket showed at least one tour in Vietnam. There were a couple of medals for valor, an Air Medal and the Silver Star, which suggested that the man knew the score and had seen some action.

They stopped long enough to get Bolan's bag from the baggage claim area. Once that was finished, they moved out into the heat of the afternoon and across a parking lot filled with baking cars, many of them with stickers for Fort Bragg.

Warringer opened the passenger's door. Bolan reached around to unlock the back and threw his bag into the rear, then climbed into the front. Warringer slid behind the wheel and started the engine. "We'll need to roll the windows down until the air conditioner kicks in. Otherwise we'll fry."

As they drove toward the post, Bolan began to feel strange. A nostalgia for a time long past. Maybe a simpler time when the issues were more black-and-white. The major violence was being committed on battlefields half a world away. While you might not be able to tell the Vietcong from the civilian villagers, you at least knew that everyone was an enemy. It made you alert to the threat, and there were safe havens. Almost anywhere outside of South Vietnam was a place where a man could travel without fear of being shot, knifed or attacked. There were areas he knew where trouble brewed, and if he felt like trouble, he could enter them. Otherwise he stuck to the lighted streets and moved without fear.

But that had all blown up with the end of the 1960s. Now everywhere could be a death trap, and a few of the passengers on a plane might decide to take all the others hostage. People traveling anywhere in the world were targets for terrorists and thugs.

The sights around him brought all that back. As they approached the main gate at Fort Bragg, which once had been little more than a guard shack where an MP in a Class A uniform waved the cars onto the base, saluting the officers, he realized just how much things had changed. The guard shack was now fortified itself, with metal barricades and fifty-five-gallon drums filled with sand. The dark glass of the shack made it hard for those approaching to see the MPs. The attacks on the Marines in Lebanon, or against American installations in West Germany, Central America and throughout the world had brought it on. A car would have a tough time crashing through the new barricades. The trusting atmosphere of the Eisenhower era was gone forever.

They stopped at the gate where Warringer, even in uniform, had to produce an ID card to prove he was a member of the military. Bolan was required to display a driver's license, and although it was from out of state, the MP thought nothing of it. Warringer had vouched for him.

"Quite a setup," Bolan remarked.

Warringer nodded as they entered the base proper. "Result of terrorist threats. We've been told we're a main target, but if we expend a little effort, the bombers and the shooters will have to go elsewhere." He shrugged. "I don't understand how making them go elsewhere is a solution, but it makes it a little safer here. We're alert to the threat, so we're a harder nut to crack."

"And the others?"

"Well, they know of the threat as well and should be as prepared. Maybe if everyone toughens up, then the terrorists will go to another country."

Bolan turned and looked out the window. The barracks erected temporarily during the Second World War still stood. Some had been converted to offices with air conditioners stuck in the windows. Others were vacant. Soldiers in fatigues worked around them, painting rocks that lined the walkways and policing the area, picking up trash and litter. Years earlier it would have been an all-male crew, but now there were a number of women working alongside the men.

Other areas of the base had been refurbished: set amid manicured lawns lined with flowers and bushes were brick buildings with smoked-glass windows and massive rooftop air conditioners. The parking lots were full of the newest cars. There was a new PX that looked as if it had been modeled after a discount department store. A hundred people, many towing kids, were moving through the parking lot. Like many military bases, Fort Bragg had been turned into a self-sufficient city.

"Briefing is going to be held in the commander's conference room."

"Then we won't be going by the Special Forces area?"

"Hadn't planned on it," Warringer said. "We can swing by if you want to, but that might make us late."

"No problem," Bolan replied. "Maybe later if there's time."

He wasn't sure why he wanted to return there. In all the years since basic training and then the individual training that had led him to the Special Forces, he'd had little desire to return to those bases. He could remember them in great detail, and it didn't seem necessary to visit, as if on some kind of pilgrimage. Now that he was here, though, it might be interesting.

They pulled up in front of a big building with a huge flagpole in front of it. On both sides of the walkway there were flowers and a beautiful green lawn so lush that it looked like fur.

Warringer shut off the engine and opened his door. "This is it."

Bolan got out the other side and together they walked up to the curved porch that led to double glass doors. Warringer opened the first door and stood aside to let Bolan precede him. Then he got the inner door, too.

The interior was dim, lighted with glowing fluorescence that did little to chase the gloom. Along one wall were framed photographs of the chain of command as it descended from the President to the local commander. Another wall held a bulletin board, which listed all the newest, local regulations. One poster warned everyone that COMSEC was their job.

Warringer led Bolan along the corridor. Most of the doors were closed, though Bolan was able to get a glimpse of the civilians busily at work in some of the offices. Faint sounds of office routine leaked into the hallway: clattering typewriters, ringing telephones, rock and roll blaring from a radio.

They reached a stairway and climbed to the second floor, moving down a corridor line with pictures of the Army in action: framed prints of the Wagon Box Fight, the Hayfield Fight, in the trenches during the First World War and at Château-Thierry, and on the beaches and fronts of the Second World War.

They finally came to an ornate door that held a small sign announcing the Office of the Commanding General. Warringer opened it and stepped inside.

Three huge wooden desks faced him, each covered with papers, each bearing In and Out trays, pens and pencils and a small lamp. A woman worked behind one, a sergeant in fatigues the second and a major in Class A's the third. There was a thick carpet on the floor, green draperies at the windows and dark paneling on the walls. A waiting area sported a coffee table with magazines arranged with military precision.

The major came around his desk, holding out his hand. He was a thin man, balding, who wore no combat decorations above his pocket. There were no jump wings, either. He was obviously a college-trained staff officer who had no hands-on experience.

"In here," he said as he opened a door.

Bolan walked across the floor and stopped short, looking into the room. A large conference table stood in the center, surrounded by chairs. More chairs lined the walls. At one end was a blackboard flanked by bulletin boards. An easel stood in one corner and a lectern in the other. The American flag stood tucked into the corner with the lectern, while a projection screen was recessed into the ceiling. More Army prints lined the walls. These showed the evolution of the Army uniform.

"You sit," the major instructed, "and I'll let the general know you've arrived."

"Will he be briefing?" Bolan asked.

"Good God, no. He'll alert the briefing officer who will be here shortly." The major turned and left the room.

Warringer took one of the chairs near the wall. "You were in the Special Forces once, weren't you?"

Bolan looked at the Army sergeant. "A lifetime ago."

"Vietnam?"

"Almost two tours," Bolan replied, then fell silent, hoping the sergeant would take the hint. There was an unwritten rule that one soldier didn't ask another about his involvement in the Vietnam War. If the soldier wanted to talk, then he did.

"When were you there?"

Bolan glanced at the sergeant but let the silence grow between them as his mind returned to the humidity of Vietnam. It was a combination of the questions, the photograph that he had seen in Washington, D.C., and being at Fort Bragg again. The Vietnam experience was something he tried not to think about too often, especially with the way the soldiers had been sold out by the American government in the end, but now there was just too much of it around him. The walls of the conference room seemed to dissolve and he was standing in the red dirt of South Vietnam, sweating heavily and wishing he was back in Pittsfield.

4

It was a hot, lazy afternoon for Sergeant Mack Bolan. He'd been in camp for just over a week, resting after four days in the field. The heat and humidity of the late afternoon hung heavy in the air, making it a challenge to even move. Men who weren't on duty wore the minimum of clothing and lay in the little shade the bunkers provided, hoping for a breeze that would cool them. Flies buzzed around them incessantly, but the effort to brush them away was too much.

Bolan sat on a short sandbag wall, wearing an OD T-shirt soaked with sweat. He'd flipped his dog tags over his shoulder so that they hung down his back. He'd jammed his feet into his combat boots but hadn't bothered to lace them. Although he wore his fatigue pants, he hadn't buttoned the top button. It was just too hot to encase himself in clothes when it wasn't necessary.

Jack Martin, a corporal who had been in-country for just over two months, sat near Bolan, drinking a beer. When the two men had bought the beer, it had been cold. What remained now was warm, but neither man cared.

"How short are you?" Martin asked.

Bolan leaned back, his elbows on the top row of sandbags, and closed his eyes. He didn't have the heart to tell Martin he planned to do another tour. "Well, let me see. I make it 102 days and a wake-up. Nearly a double-digit midget."

"We'll have a party," Martin shouted, slurring his words slightly. "A big, massive party as you burst into double-digit-dom."

Bolan had to grin. "Is that a word, double-digit-dom?"

"I don't know. Hell, I don't care. I was going to say the party was for going over the hump, but hell, that was two months ago."

"About." Bolan put his beer down, balancing it on one of the rubberized sandbags. They were something new. The old ones, made of cloth and canvas, rotted quickly in the tropical weather, splitting and leaking their sand all over the ground. These were supposed to last longer.

The tropical sun sat on the horizon, casting a glow over the camp, giving it a blood-red appearance that somehow seemed appropriate. Bolan stood and suddenly realized that everything around him had gotten quiet. The sounds of the flies had disappeared, the conversations that had carried to his position were gone and the radios had been shut off. The raucous cries of the birds had fallen silent. It was as if they were in the eye of the storm waiting for the hurricane to swoop in on them, leveling everything and killing everyone.

Bolan took one hesitant step down the hill and froze. He glanced around, wondering what was about to happen. Without understanding why, he dropped to the ground and began crawling rapidly toward his tent. No one seemed to think it strange.

The single shot was fired from a long way off, and the report of the weapon was dulled by the distance. Bolan began to crawl faster, wanting to get to his equipment. The spotting scope might give him a chance to find the enemy sniper. A rippling of rifle shots came from the south side of the perimeter, and a machine gun began to chatter.

Bolan reached his tent. He plucked his rifle from his cot and returned outside, heading toward the perimeter. As he approached, the firing tapered off. There were shouts, cries for medics and the pop of rotor blades as a helicopter gunship hovered over the jungle, searching for the sniper.

At the perimeter Bolan sat up and peeked over a short wall of sandbags. He used the scope on his weapon to search the tree lines four and five hundred meters away. The only movement was from a squad that had been outside manning the LPs—listening posts—and who were now sweeping toward the west, looking for the enemy. The mortar tubes on the east side of the camp fired, sending a volley exploding into the trees.

Bolan got to his feet as others ran up to him. A lieutenant stood on top of a bunker using binoculars as he searched for the sniper. Maybe he was trying to draw fire in the grandstand play, but it wasn't working.

Bolan slipped on the safety and slung his weapon. As he walked back up the hill to where he'd left Corporal Martin, he realized that the buzz he'd received from the beer was gone. He was stone-cold sober.

The flurry of activity where Martin waited caught his eye. Bolan ran forward and saw the body lying in the red mud. Blood stained the hands and clothes of several of the men kneeling there. Two of the soldiers were shouting instructions, while four or five others rooted to the spot, their faces pale as if they were scared.

"Jack!" Bolan couldn't see his friend, and there was a sinking feeling in his stomach as he ran forward.

The bullet had caught Martin in the throat, severing the carotid artery. He was slumped on his side, blood covering his face and hands and turning his uniform a rusty brown. A beer can lay near his outstretched hand, looking as if he had tried to reach it before he died.

"Jack..." Bolan whispered. He looked into the faces of the medics, but didn't need their confirmation. There was so much blood splattered around, and Martin's skin had taken on a pasty whiteness as if it had been bleached.

"Sorry, Sergeant," one of the medics said. "He was dead before he hit the ground. No way we could stop the bleeding anyway."

Without a word, Bolan returned to his tent. He stripped off his T-shirt and replaced it with a jungle jacket, then picked up his webgear and slipped into it. He strapped his rucksack on tightly and buckled his pistol belt. Although his canteen was empty now, he could fill it before he left the perimeter. His helmet sat on the floor, but he ignored it, preferring the boonie hat that would shade his eyes but not strain his muscles with the extra weight.

He headed for the TOC—Tactical Operations Center—a bunker near the center of the camp that directed all the activities around the perimeter. He entered through a Z-shaped doorway designed to keep shrapnel and bullets out. The interior was lighted by red bulbs hung from bare wires. The thick plank floor was covered with a thin coating of dirt. Dust seemed to hang in the air, giving everything an unnatural look. Radios and field phones were stacked at the rear, the link that kept the men inside in touch with the men on the perimeter, on patrol and at the main headquarters thirty kilometers away. The red and green lights glowed brightly, and the needles danced on the VU meters.

A group of officers worked over a map at the table in the center of the TOC. Each was dressed in fatigues, but only the highest ranking men were wearing starched uniforms. The lower ranking officers wore dirty, wrinkled ones. Bolan approached them. He stopped near the head of the table, but didn't say anything.

"What's up, Mack?" asked the lieutenant who had been standing on the bunker searching for the enemy earlier.

"I'm going out."

"I don't think that's such a good idea."

"I know who that sniper was. It had to be the Rifleman. He's the only one with the balls to come here to shoot. We've been chasing him for two months, and it's time to end it. I'm going out."

The conversation stopped as all the officers looked at Bolan, but only the young lieutenant spoke to him.

"Let's wait until morning. You won't be able to find the trail in the dark."

"We need to throw out a couple of patrols and chase him and his security around," Bolan said. "Keep them so busy running from us that they don't have the time to cover their tracks or go to ground."

The lieutenant turned and looked at the starched and pressed major. "Sir?"

"If Sergeant Bolan thinks he can accomplish something out there tonight, then, by all means, let him go. Security squad ready?"

"No, sir," Bolan replied. "I don't think I want them. They slow me down and give the enemy warning that we're in the area. Once I pick up the trail, I don't want to have to worry about a bunch of amateurs."

"I'm not sure I like your attitude very much, Sergeant."

"Excuse me, sir, but we're wasting time."

The major looked from man to man and then at the map on the table. "Where are you going?"

Bolan leaned forward and stabbed the map with his finger. "Here. That's where I've run into this guy before. It's his AO, so he'll stick close to it. I'll find a blind along this ridge and settle in to wait."

"Draw a radio and stay in touch. If you don't see anything in three days, you're back in here. We have need for your talents on other missions."

"Yes, sir."

"And, Sergeant, good luck. I hope you smoke the bastard."

"Thank you, Major."

Bolan whirled and hurried from the TOC before anyone thought to ask about who his spotter would be. This was going to be a one-man job, and Bolan didn't want to clutter it up with a lot of unnecessary thought caused by

Army bureaucracy. All that was needed was one man out in the bush, waiting for the enemy to show himself, without a lot of others around him to screw it up.

He reached the wooden-and-wire gate in the perimeter, which was guarded by two bunkers that housed a .50-caliber machine gun each and four M-60s. Those were flanked by two other bunkers that held a squad apiece, making the gate the strongest point on the perimeter. If Charlie attacked, he would come up on the opposite side, blowing holes in the wire with satchel charges to reach the bunker line.

Bolan crouched at the side of the bunker guarding the gate, waiting for complete darkness. From the inside he could hear the quiet voices of the men as they discussed women. He couldn't understand the words because the voices were too quiet, but he knew what the topic would be. It was always women.

Beyond the wire there were fleeting shapes in the growing darkness. The squads were out there, searching for the enemy, hoping to keep Charlie off balance. They were making noise and were visible, in the belief that the Vietcong would flee the area now that the attack was over. Bolan hoped the squads wouldn't be ambushed, which was a possibility that no one in the TOC seemed to have considered.

When the shapes faded, and before the flares were fired to illuminate the perimeter, Bolan slipped through the wire. He moved rapidly, working his way to the west where he believed the sniper had hidden. The Vietcong sniper—called simply the Rifleman—would have to have been there to have killed Martin. The search was taking place too far to the east, which suited Bolan fine.

He stopped briefly when he reached the edge of the perimeter, his eyes on the tree line now just over two hundred meters away. The field of short elephant grass showed numerous trails, the majority made by American patrols from the camp. There were no clues there.

Keeping low, trying not to silhouette himself against the light-colored red dust of the camp, Bolan crept through the grass, trying not to leave a trail, though he doubted Charlie would be around to spot it.

When he reached the trees, he stopped and knelt on one knee. With his left hand he touched the rough bark of a palm and listened carefully. The only sounds from the jungle were natural. Birds, lizards, monkeys and insects.

The warrior got to his feet and entered the tree line, working his way through it carefully, putting the heel of his foot down and slowly rotating it toward the toe so that he made no noise. He intended to work his way through the trees like a wraith. No one would hear him. And when he finally surfaced he would be a deadly surprise.

From the east came the sounds of men—not much noise, just the rustle of cloth against leaves or the snap of a twig that was barely audible. A single, muffled cough caused Bolan to go down on one knee next to a wet fern. He felt the water soak through his sleeve.

The squad appeared moments later, little more than charcoal shapes moving against a flat black background. It was the movement that gave them away. Bolan stared at them, picking up the distinctive shapes of their weapons—M-14s mostly, but a couple of the newer M-16s, too. Bolan let the soldiers pass without a word to them, and although they were no more than two meters away, no one suspected he was there.

When the squad had disappeared, he began his journey again. By midnight, he was through the tree line and had reached the open country on the other side of it. He skirted the open fields and rice paddies, staying just inside the trees where it would be difficult, if not impossible, for the enemy to spot him—if the enemy was there looking.

He stopped once to rest. Sweat soaked his uniform, turning it as black as the night. Insects that had been bothering him earlier seemed to have lost interest. He sipped from his canteen, not wanting to drink much of his limited supply of water. A single capful was all he allowed himself, knowing that his sweating would steal the water from him quickly.

It was nearly two in the morning when he reached the ridgeline. He climbed upward until he was at the military crest, a point just below the summit where he could walk without silhouetting himself against the sky.

He circled around, now moving to the south, all the while staying on the ridgeline. After three or four kilometers, he began to search for a blind. He descended and then climbed a small hill that dominated the surrounding countryside. A shallow depression about three-quarters of the way up the hill deepened into a gully and then turned so that it pointed downhill. Partly shielded by rock from the top of the hill, it gave a commanding view of the valley, rice paddies and fields for several kilometers. Bolan decided to use it and see what it looked like in the morning.

When dawn came, Bolan was ready. He had his binoculars out and was sweeping the field, memorizing everything he could see: farmers' hootches tucked into small groves of palm trees; a mud wall that ran from one hootch toward a water buffalo corral six meters away; a network of rice paddy dikes; a thin tree line that followed the course of a meandering river; a few bushes and lone trees that suggested something more sinister. The Vietcong often disguised their spider holes and tunnel entrances with plants, but the floor of the valley had so few that they looked obvious. Bolan didn't care. He'd watch them all, waiting for the enemy to appear.

As the valley came awake, farmers moving toward their fields, women beginning fires to cook the morning meal, Bolan pulled out a tin of crackers. He used his P-38 to open the crackers and a tin of runny jelly. Keeping one eye on the valley, he ate his morning meal and then buried the cans so that they wouldn't give him away.

There was movement at the edge of the valley, and the warrior turned to see two men break cover, heading toward the tree line along the river, a good six or seven hundred meters from them.

Through the binoculars he could tell nothing about them. They were dressed in black pajamas and wore the conical coolie hats that everyone wore. Nothing distinguished them from the other farmers spreading into the valley, except they didn't wear sandals. Even at that distance Bolan could see they wore some kind of boot or high-topped shoe, and that meant NVA, not VC.

He had taken a chance, leapfrogged forward and hoped to put himself between the Rifleman and his sanctuary. Apparently his second-guessing of the enemy had been successful.

When the two men reached the mud wall, they halted and disappeared. A moment later one of them popped up at the far end, near the hootch, where a woman now stood with her back to the wall. She appeared to be frightened, though the man didn't seem to be threatening her.

Now the whole squad broke cover, working its way toward the mud wall. There was no longer a question about the identities of the men. This group carried weapons and moved like a military formation. Bolan put down his binoculars and picked up his rifle, popping the lens cap. He sighted, then checked the wind by watching the drifting smoke from the cooking fire. It was almost dead calm.

When the squad was halfway to its destination, Bolan aimed at the last man in the line. He checked the range and the wind again, then waited for an opportunity to get off a shot. The idea was to pin the enemy behind the mud wall close to the hootch where he could take his time picking them off one by one until he killed them all or the sniper showed himself.

As the team approached the wall, it stopped for a moment, and Bolan fired. The report of his weapon was lost in the distance. The enemy heard nothing.

The round drilled the last man, dropping him in his tracks. From the way he fell, Bolan knew the guy was dead. The man nearest to him turned, saw his fellow lying in the mud and rushed back. As he crouched over the body, Bolan fired again. The slug slammed into the man's back, flipping him onto the first victim.

A third NVA turned and saw the others in the mud. His shout alerted the squad, and as he took a step to the rear, Bolan dropped him. That started a panic. The others sprinted for the mud wall, leaving the dead where they had fallen. Rifle shots rang out, but they were fired indiscriminately as the enemy tried to get Bolan to make a mistake and reveal himself.

Instead, the Executioner set his weapon aside and used his binoculars again. The three men he'd picked off were dead. There was blood all over the place. None of them had moved since being shot, and Bolan wondered if he should have tried to wound one of them. It was an old trick. Wound a man and then pick off the heroes who tried to rescue him.

The rifle fire tapered off as the enemy realized they were doing nothing more than wasting ammunition. The farmers had disappeared from the fields, and the women had run into the hootches. No one was going to move until Bolan decided it was time for them to move.

He picked up his canteen and took a mouthful of water. The sun had been up for nearly two hours, but the shadows of the depression protected him, leaving him in the shade. It would be a hot, miserable day, but worse for the NVA on the valley floor. The mud wall would offer them little in the way of protection from the sun, and they would get brave after a while, giving Bolan the chance to take out more of them.

But Bolan realized something as he sat there watching for movement. As he replayed the confrontation in his mind, he discovered that not one of the NVA was carrying a long-range rifle. Each had an AK-47 or an SKS, but no one had the Mosin-Nagant that the enemy used for sniping. Therefore the Rifleman was not with these men.

That didn't mean this team wasn't his security squad. Bolan sometimes was separated from his squad by a kilometer or more, and they didn't reunite until they were all nearly back at camp. If these men were security for the Rifleman, then the sniper was out there somewhere, lying in a blind, waiting for Bolan to make a mistake. It would become a war of nerves, with the NVA behind the mud wall being used as pawns by both men.

Bolan rolled to the right, staying in the shadows of the depression, and used his binoculars. He began a slow search of the tree lines and hillsides around him, searching for the Rifleman. The enemy sniper was well trained and would know how to select his blind. Occasionally he turned his glasses on the mud wall and hootch where the NVA soldiers were pinned down, but so far no one had been inclined to move.

By noon everything in the valley had slowed to a standstill. The farmers had returned to their fields when the shooting had stopped, but had now abandoned them because of the heat. Still there was no breeze, and Bolan felt the sweat rolling down his body. If he had been caught in the open, with no relief from the sun, the heat would have been almost intolerable. Even in the shade he was beginning to bake.

The first movement from below came a few minutes later. One man rose, as if to make himself a target, but then dropped down immediately. It was the old hat-on-a-stick trick. Bolan didn't fall for it.

Minutes later it happened again, and then one man stood deliberately, exposing himself. He disappeared a second later, and although Bolan had a good shot at him, he didn't take it. Now was the time to be selective.

He sipped his water and dribbled a little down the back of his neck, which seemed to cool his whole body. A fly hovered around his face, darting at his eyes, but Bolan ignored the insect. Unnecessary movement told the enemy where you were. Each motion was made slowly, cautiously, and each was planned before it was executed.

The enemy apparently had taken as much of the heat as they could. Now that the sniper had stopped shooting at them, they decided it was time to get out. One man stood and sprinted to the hootch, diving through the doorway. He reappeared a moment later, crouched in the semidarkness, his weapon held at the ready. Bolan decided he should be rewarded for his bravery and didn't shoot him.

A second man appeared and ran by the hootch. He leaped into a rice paddy, splashing dirty water everywhere. Although he tried to crouch behind the protection of the dike, part of his back and legs were visible.

It was obvious they were trying to reach the trees along the river. Once there they would have all the cover they needed to escape. Bolan decided he wouldn't give them the chance. Besides, if they were the Rifleman's security, he would be somewhere close.

Bolan aimed at the man lying in the rice paddy. He again checked the wind and saw that a slight breeze had picked up, but it was blowing more or less in his face. He put the cross hairs on the man and then adjusted them. He took a deep breath, exhaled and took another, holding half of it.

Just as he fired, the man in the rice paddy looked up. The round struck him in the center of the forehead, blowing off the back of his skull in a spray of blood and brain. The muscles spasmed, and the man flipped over the dike. His legs drummed in the water, splashing it into a froth. He waved his arms for a moment and then collapsed completely, the blood spreading over the water in a giant red halo.

Rifle fire erupted again, but the enemy still had no idea where Bolan was. They got off a few shots, again hoping Bolan would reveal his position. But Bolan didn't shoot. It was time to let them stew again. Time to let them wait for death to strike like lightning from the unseen enemy.

THE DOOR to the conference room opened, drawing Bolan's attention to the present, and another man entered. He clutched a green beret in one hand and had a briefcase in the other. He wore jump wings and a combat infantryman's badge and had more than a dozen ribbons given for valor. This wasn't one of the many cardboard officers who inhabited the ranks of the modern Army. Here was a man, like Warringer, who knew the score.

He stepped to the head of the table and then looked around the empty room. As he sat down, he said, "Given us more space than we need. Wish they would do this all the time. I'm Colonel Moore. How are you doing, Warringer?"

"Fine, sir."

"You must be Bolan."

"Right."

The colonel studied the Executioner for a moment, staring hard into his eyes "I've heard of you."

"Yes, sir."

Moore opened his briefcase and took out a folder. "I guess it's time we got down to business. The information included in this briefing is classified. I don't want to read it in the newspaper tonight. That clear?"

"You don't have to worry about me talking out of turn," Bolan said dryly.

"No, I don't suppose I do. Now, if I can have your undivided attention, I'll try to get you out of here in time for dinner."

5

McDonald sat across the table from Rachel Jamison and wished he had insisted they return to his house rather than waste time eating dinner in a restaurant. He could have cooked something for them if Rachel felt she had to have something to eat. It seemed that everything in the restaurant was moving at slow motion. The maître d' had kept them waiting for a table, the wine steward had been slow and the waiter seemed to be crippled. No one was in a hurry, and even after they had ordered the meal, it seemed as if an eternity had passed before the food arrived.

Rachel wasn't helping, either. All the way to the restaurant she had flirted with him. She had tugged at the hem of her skirt to draw his attention to her thighs and then let it ride high, showing off her shapely legs. In conversation she had touched him repeatedly and she had leaned close a number of times, letting her perfume wash over him, enveloping him in a sweet-smelling cloud. Now, at the table, she continued the game. Her blouse was unbuttoned at the throat so that he could catch glimpses of her breasts as she talked to him. Once, she had brought her elbows together to deepen the cleavage and then had grinned when she'd caught him staring down her shirt.

So, McDonald picked at his food, his appetite destroyed by the game she played. Rachel, on the other hand, consumed everything placed in front of her. She ate it slowly, drawing out the meal while McDonald suffered the ache in his crotch. He wanted to get out of the restaurant and to his house. He wanted to rip her clothes off and throw her to the floor, taking only time to inspect her flawless body quickly before he relieved his hunger. That done, he would savor her, working with her until they were both satisfied. But that was for later.

When the waiter finally brought the check, McDonald nearly threw the money at him. He restrained himself as they walked from the restaurant into the sultry evening. The streets were crowded, but McDonald didn't notice the pedestrians. He was vaguely aware of the night sounds—blaring horns in the distance, the roar of a jet overhead, which was reminiscent of the war in Vietnam when aircraft were returning from air strikes against the Vietcong. Thoughts of Ryan surfaced, but McDonald pushed them aside. When he was with a beautiful woman, he didn't want to think about some dumb agent who had gotten himself lost in Vietnam.

He wanted to suggest that they go to the car, that the night was too humid for walking, but Rachel pulled him along, as if she had a destination in mind. McDonald felt the sweat blossom on his body and trickle down his back and sides. He thought of her, the sheen of sweat covering her body as she thrust herself at him, and he felt his desire rise again. The beads of sweat forming between her breasts and sliding down to the softness of her belly were erotic. He wanted to lick the sweat from her body, and it took a great deal of effort to stifle the urge. There was nothing he could do on the streets of Bangkok.

They walked along the Sawankhalok that bordered the Royal Turf Club and crossed Si Ayutthaya so that they were looking at the park where the Chitlada Palace stood. Rachel pulled McDonald into the shadows and held him tightly.

"You like me?" she asked huskily.

"Oh, yes," he said. "Very much. More than I care to admit."

She rewarded him with a kiss, and all thoughts of the daily grind, of Ryan, deserted him. He was aware only of her, her body and the dampness of her skin against his fingers as he tried to reach inside her blouse to touch her breasts.

"We walk some more, I think," she said. "We walk so that we are not full from our dinner."

McDonald didn't want to walk. He wanted to see if the ground was as soft as it looked and if they could find a place where they wouldn't be disturbed, but knew that he couldn't. There were too many people in Bangkok, and the last thing he needed was to be arrested by the local police. He released his grip on Rachel and let her drag him back into the light.

Again she grinned at him mischievously. "What did you do today?"

McDonald shrugged. "Not too much."

She took his hand and pulled him along the street, heading in the general direction of the Amphawan Garden. There were other people around them, but McDonald felt as though they were the only two people in the universe.

"You do nothing?" she asked, sounding as if she were disappointed in him.

"Well, today I didn't do all that much," he said. "Just sat in my office and read reports."

"What sort of reports?" she persisted, tugging at him so that his arm brushed her breast.

It was a game they played often. She asked him questions, as if he were her husband and were home after a hard day at the office. He denied doing anything important, but slowly she got the information out of him, learning about the sorry state of the world.

"Reports of the contras in Nicaragua. They've been pushing hard, trying to force their government into general elections."

"Just as happened in Cambodia," she replied.

"Well, it's not really the same thing. Kind of a reverse situation."

They reached the Misakawan Garden and turned again, now heading in the general direction of the car. They walked in silence for a while. McDonald was aware of the softness of her hip as it bumped into him periodically. He was aware of the swell of her breast as she touched his arm while holding his hand. He was aware of the total woman as they reached the car. He opened the door and watched her get in, refusing to avert his eyes during the awkward moment when she revealed more of her legs than she wanted.

He hurried around to the other side and climbed behind the wheel. When he had started the engine, he glanced to the rear and then pulled into traffic.

Rachel slipped across the seat so that she was sitting next to him, her thigh and hip against his, her shoulder touching his chest. He put an arm around her shoulders, letting his fingers touch her breast. She sighed with pleasure.

"Whatever happened to that man who sneaked into Vietnam?"

McDonald kept his eyes on the road. He felt her respond to him. "Still nothing. He just disappeared as if he had fallen off the face of the earth."

"Anyone going to go look for him?"

"You sure have an interest in that man."

"I just wondered what was going to happen next, now that he is missing."

"Well, as it stands," McDonald responded, "nothing is being planned, but I doubt the situation will stay that way long. Someone is going to have to go in and see if they can find him, if only to answer a few questions."

She shuddered. "It won't be you, will it?"

"Ah, so now I understand your interest in this. No, it won't be me. I've advanced far beyond fieldwork. Oh, in an emergency, I would head out, but this is no emergency. Someone else will be dispatched. Hell, he may even coordinate through my office."

McDonald pulled to the side of the road and parked. "We're here," he announced.

She sat up and looked around and then said, "Oh, I'm sorry, but I have to go home. My mother is expecting me early. She insisted that I come straight home."

"But..."

"Be a dear. It was the only way I could convince her that nothing was going on. She's so suspicious of everything since my father deserted her and returned to England."

"Rachel, I'm not sure I can take this."

She touched his chest gently, letting her hand drop lower. "I'm sorry, but I'll make it up to you. I promise. Anything you want, you shall have."

"That gives me a lot of leeway."

She kissed his cheek. "But I trust you. You'd never do anything to harm me."

THE SCREAMING FROM THE CAGE was beginning to grate on Diem's nerves. At first it hadn't been too bad, an occasional wail that cut through the evening, but this had been going on far too long. It wasn't that Diem was developing humanitarian ideas; he feared the prisoner would die before giving up all his secrets.

Leaving the remains of his dinner, Diem pushed himself from his desk and stood. He went into his quarters, washed himself and then selected a clean uniform. Every time he visited the prisoner, he wore a fresh uniform for the psychological advantage it gave him. Shined shoes and polished brass completed the picture. The poor man, covered in filth, wearing rags, saw his captor looking as fresh as ever. It was one more weapon against him.

Feeling better, Diem hurried from his hootch as the screaming became a continuous roar of pain. He burst through the door in dramatic fashion and demanded in English, "What the hell is going on here?"

The two guards leaped back, away from Ryan, who slipped to the floor and rolled onto his side. He hiked up his knees and moaned quietly. Blood spread over his bandages where his wounds had been reopened. Cuts and bruises covered his face, and one eye was swollen shut. The guards had done their job well.

Maximum pain and damage with little danger that Ryan would die in the near future.

When neither guard answered the question, Diem shouted at them. "Get out of here. I don't want you near this man again. Do you hear me?"

One of the guards replied in English, "But, Comrade Colonel, the prisoner refuses to cooperate. There is information that we need."

"I don't care," Diem snarled. "Get out of here. Now."

He crouched near Ryan and asked if he could sit up. Although the whole conversation had taken place in English, the agent didn't seem to notice. If Ryan hadn't been so sick from his wounds and in such pain from the beating, Diem would never have tried such a transparent trick.

He helped Ryan into a sitting position and then eased him onto the cot. He poked at the wounds, clucking with concern, then said, "You're going to need some medical help very soon."

Ryan said nothing. He stared at the floor, coughed and spit blood onto the rough-hewn wood.

"Medical help," Diem repeated. "But to get that help, I need something from you. You have to provide some information. Not that nonsense about a sightseeing tour of the places in Vietnam where you had fought. If that was the case, you could have applied for a visa. You didn't have to sneak over the border like a common criminal."

Still Ryan didn't speak. He rocked back so that he was leaning against the bamboo that formed the bars on the inside of the hootch. He drew up his knees and sat quietly.

"We can let you die and no one would know. You would be just another of the many missing in Southeast Asia." Diem noticed a reaction to the statement. "Oh. Maybe we're getting somewhere. Missing in action."

"Not here for that." Ryan's words were slow and hard to understand. His lips were split and swollen from the recent beating.

"You are obviously an American. Tell me where you hid your passport and who helped you get across the border."

"No help."

"Ah, but that cannot be true. You must have come through Thailand, and you could not have gotten across Kampuchea without help."

"Parachute."

"Good. Where is the chute?"

"Burned."

"Not so good. I need proof. You tell me something, and I'll see what I can do to get you medical assistance. But you lie to me, and I'll not be able to do a thing for you. There are others who will report me to my headquarters if I don't have something to show them."

Ryan took a deep breath and wheezed. He began to cough and pain doubled him over.

"This is all so unnecessary," Diem said. "A little assistance, a show of good faith, and I can get you all that you need. Why torture yourself?"

"Thailand," Ryan replied. "Two people from a camp. They lead. Once here, they return. In Thailand again."

"Good. Very good. Now where is your passport and your papers?" Diem noticed that the parachute story had been forgotten already. With no parachute to find, the story had evaporated.

"Thailand. Nothing to identify me."

"Your name?"

"Thomas Ryan."

"And you are an American, sent by the CIA to spy on the Vietnamese people and maybe prepare some invasion reports?"

"No. Just look around."

"Anything that you wanted to see? Some special mission that you were on?"

Ryan shook his head slowly. His sweat- and blood-soaked hair hung in his face, and his breath came slowly, whistling through his split lips and broken teeth.

"See how life is now. See changes."

Diem snorted. "That's a lie. We've invited American journalists to Vietnam. Your CBS newspeople came in 1984 to see how the revolution has improved the quality of life."

"Staged trip. This for real."

Diem reached out and patted Ryan on the leg. "You've done very good tonight. A little white lie at the end can be tolerated, considering all that you've said." Diem moved to the door and was handed a bucket of water by the guard stationed just outside the hootch. He returned to Ryan and used the dipper to give him some of it to drink.

Ryan looked up at him. "Need doctor."

"Well, I'm sorry about that, but we don't have a doctor. We have some medicine here, and we'll do

what we can for you. You'll just have to get some rest
and hope for the best.''

"I don't get back, someone will come. Come looking for me."

Diem couldn't help but smile. "I know that someone will come. We'll just have to hope he does a better job of it than you have."

MOORE HELD on to his briefing folder for a moment,
then handed it over to Bolan. "That will tell you
everything you need to know."

Bolan accepted the folder and opened it to reveal a
thick report, a series of maps and more than a dozen
aerial photographs. He glanced through them quickly,
then looked at the report. He dropped it back onto the
table without reading it. "This isn't the way I work."

"I understand that," Moore admitted. "But we
want to lay all the cards on the table, give you the information we have to ensure the success of your mission."

Bolan shook his head. "I was told all this in Washington. There was no need for me to come to Fort
Bragg to be told the same things."

"Mr. Bolan, I'm in charge of this mission. What
you learned in Washington was only the preliminary.
We're getting to the meat of the problem here."

Bolan realized it would do no good to argue with the
man. Moore believed he was right, and there was no
way to convince him it was a waste of time and tax-
payers' money to fly Bolan to Bragg. No one in the
government cared about the cost because it wasn't
money from their pockets. That was the reason every

program needed money: to bankroll all the bureaucrats who were building empires.

To satisfy the colonel, Bolan picked up the typed report and glanced through it. The text was nothing more than a listing of all the sightings of men suspected of being held prisoner in Southeast Asia, suggesting that Americans were still being held by the Vietnamese. There was a cautious statement about Robert Garwood, the Marine who was court-martialed in 1979 for collaborating with the enemy. But there was no definitive proof, just as Hal Brognola had said earlier.

Bolan flipped through the report, which suggested the sites of the prisoner camps, many of them in Laos and North Vietnam, which were considered too far from friendly territory. For some reason the government felt that clandestine missions into either of those places would somehow fail, even though the Special Forces and the Navy's SEALs had worked in North Vietnam frequently during the war.

Moore, who had been quietly smoking a cigarette, finally spoke up. "This is the first indication of white men in the Saigon area. We had thousands of men around Saigon during the war, so there isn't a thing we don't know about it."

"Except that the information is fifteen years out-of-date."

"But things haven't changed that much. We can tell that from the aerial reconnaissance of the area."

Bolan pulled the photos closer and examined them. One showed the remnants of the big American camp at Cu Chi. When the Americans had pulled out, the local population had swooped in, stealing everything they could get their hands on. Then the North Vietnamese army had taken over and turned the camp into a reeducation center. The fences had been pulled forward, surrounding a smaller area, but they could be seen. The scars left by the bigger base were obvious from the air.

"Now, Mr. Bolan, there are a few ground rules under which we're going to have to operate. These were designed with your protection in mind."

"You're beginning to talk me out of this."

Moore smiled at that. "Please, hear me out. I think you'll see the wisdom of this. Your cover will be of a tourist going to visit the sights in Bangkok and to take in the nightlife. You'll have to arrive without weapons and find them on the black market. Any effort we make to clear you through customs with weapons is going to draw attention to you. There's no real problem finding weapons in Bangkok, and we think that using the black market will draw less attention to you. Our assumption is that the first man in was picked up by the Vietnamese and that happened because of leaks in the Bangkok embassy. The way was paved for him. We eliminate that step, and you become one of thousands of Americans arriving in Bangkok every month." Moore pulled the file closer. "You will be given a number of contacts there, people who can be trusted. It's up to you to use them."

"Seems to me that the fewer people who know why I'm there, the better off I'm going to be."

"Yes," Moore agreed, "there is something to that. Now, let me brief you on the rest of this, and we can get you onto the airplane."

Bolan dragged the picture of the camp closer to him and studied it carefully. The terrain around it was fairly flat. No real hills. A few gentle slopes that were ten, twelve feet above the surrounding fields. Tree lines crisscrossed the area, providing some cover. The Hobo Woods were to the northeast, and beyond that the Song Sai Gon, or the Saigon River. Michelin used to have a rubber plantation near Dau Tieng, and Bolan wondered if it was still there.

His route from the border would have to be north of Highway One. The ground to the south was either too open or too swampy. It would only be a matter of hours before he was spotted. A parachute drop would make the whole operation that much easier, and he said as much to Moore.

"That was a consideration, but then we didn't want to overfly the territory because it could alert the enemy. The population in the area is heavy enough that someone would probably see you land. The overland route contains the fewest risks."

Bolan glanced at Moore's chest again and read the medals he saw there. Enough combat awards to suggest he knew something of the life of a soldier on the ground, knew the hardships of moving through enemy territory without making a sound. He should understand the constant strain of being silent, of watching where you stepped, and of not leaving anything behind. Now he was talking about a walk across two countries as if it were a stroll through the park.

Moore was off again, talking of the mission in great detail, outlining everything Bolan would have to know before he hit the target. Bolan, on the other hand, was thinking of Vietnam. Not the beautiful country of deep, garden greens and brightly colored flowers, but the country ripped by war as soldiers from both armies searched for one another.

He thought of the mud wall where the security squad crouched, hiding from the sniper who killed everyone who tried to get away.

6

By late afternoon Bolan had shot another three NVA soldiers. Two of them had tried to run into the jungle to the west, heading back the way they had come, and the other had popped up near the center of the wall, using a pair of binoculars. Bolan had put the cross hairs on the man's face and fired one round. The binoculars had erupted into the air as the man had disappeared behind the mud wall.

There had been no return fire that time. No one had peeked over the wall to shoot back, and no one had tried to run to the bodies of the men who had been shot. They were content to wait until dark. With patience, they would be able to slip away after sunset.

One of the NVA was crawling along a dike, using the water as a cover so that only a small part of his body showed. He kept his head down, peeking up periodically to check his position and to breathe.

The shot would be so simple that Bolan almost felt guilty about it. He wondered if he was reacting to his role as a sniper. In every war movie he'd seen, the snipers were considered second-class enemy soldiers who fired from hiding, killing the fun-loving Americans. Sniping was something that Americans didn't do. The enemy did it.

But Bolan knew that such feelings were ridiculous. Sniping at the enemy was as old as war itself. One sniper could pin down a battalion, if the terrain was right and he knew what he was doing. Snipers had been employed as the rear guard a hundred times so that the main body of a trapped force could get away.

There were military men who looked down on the snipers as if they were something less than human. But these same men had no remorse when they called in artillery or an air strike. The sniper had a specific target, and innocent men and women weren't killed by them. An air strike could wipe out a whole village, killing everyone whether he or she was the enemy or not.

It was a question that Bolan had thought about frequently as he'd gone through the specialized sniper training. It was a question that was addressed by the instructors, making each man understand that a sniper was a highly trained professional, better at most military skills than his friends. Snipers operated in small groups or alone, so they had to be the best.

A sniper wasn't a cowardly soldier who hid in the grass killing indiscriminately. He was a highly trained soldier whose skills inflicted great damage on specific enemy soldiers. If the VC or NVA knew that they were in an area where snipers operated successfully, the VC and NVA would go elsewhere.

Bolan drove the thoughts from his mind. War was killing the enemy and inflicting damage. That was all it was. When enough people had died and enough damage inflicted, the war ended. That was the only way. Snipers were just a very effective way to achieve that end.

So Bolan rolled onto his stomach, wrapped the sling of his rifle around his arm, drawing it tight, then sighted on the man far below him. He got a good look at the man who thought he was being so clever. The enemy soldier reached a dike and stopped moving. Lying quietly there, resting, he looked like a bit of wood floating in the water. It was hard to identify him as an enemy soldier.

Bolan put the cross hairs on the man's back, then checked the wind. It was still blowing at him. Again he went through the breathing ritual, preparing himself to fire. He squeezed the trigger, felt the weapon slam back and heard the bang of the report.

Just as he shot, the man in the paddy moved slightly, but not enough. The bullet struck him low in the back, between the hips. He jerked once and then rolled over, his hands grabbing at the loose vegetation on top of the dike as if he were trying to drag himself out of the water. He clawed at the dirt but failed to heave himself out.

Through the scope Bolan could see the man's mouth working as he shouted for help. The kind thing would be to put another bullet into the man and end his pain. Bolan worked the bolt and aimed again, but as he did, firing broke out from behind the wall. It wasn't the random shooting that had happened before. Now it was directed toward him. The rounds either hit low, kicking up dirt on the hillside, or passed harmlessly overhead. The enemy hadn't found the range and, given their AK-47s or their SKSs, they wouldn't be much of a threat to him, anyway.

Bolan sighted on the wall and waited. One man shifted around so that a shoulder was exposed. Bolan aimed at it and fired. A moment later the man dropped his weapon and disappeared behind the wall. It wasn't a kill, but the soldier was wounded. One less man for him to worry about.

And then there was a snapping sound above his head, not the distant popping from the poorly aimed AKs, but something that came close, like a bee buzzing by his ear. There was a thud to the rear, and then a ricochet as the bullet hit the rock. Chips flew up like shrapnel from a grenade. That had been closer than it should have been.

Instinctively he turned toward the trees nearly twelve hundred meters away. Using the scope of his weapon, he searched for the enemy sniper, sure that the Rifleman had finally appeared to save what was left of his security squad. But there was no movement that showed him where the enemy hid.

While Bolan searched, the men behind the mud wall kept shooting, burning through their ammo quickly. Bolan didn't worry about it. None of the rounds came very close to him.

As he watched, he saw a flash of light, and when he turned toward it he thought he saw movement. Nothing much. Maybe a hand and arm working the bolt of a Mosin-Nagant sniper rifle, a flicker of movement twelve hundred meters away that hinted of the Rifleman's hiding place.

Without trying to identify more of the target, Bolan aimed and fired. He had little hope of hitting his adversary, but hoped to set him thinking. If the Rifleman knew that Bolan knew where he hid, the man might move, might expose himself, giving Bolan the opportunity to kill him.

There was no return fire, and Bolan wondered if he had lucked into a perfect shot. No movement in the trees across the valley. Firing continued along the wall, but none of that was accurate. Just noise to draw his attention.

And then Bolan realized that was exactly what it all was. They had him spotted. The men behind the wall could do nothing. Even if they rushed him, he could cut them down before they made it halfway up the hill.

But the man on the hill across the valley didn't have that problem. There were no American soldiers for him to worry about. He had a weapon that would let him fire at the same ranges Bolan used. At the moment, Bolan had the advantage because of the high ground, but if he stayed where he was, the enemy could get behind him and pin him down.

Without hesitation, Bolan slipped back from the lip of the depression and began to crawl along the gully. He moved rapidly, staying in the shadows, trying not to kick up tiny clouds of dust that would give away his position. He ignored the sun that faced him and the humidity that threatened to kill him slowly. He wiped his sweating hands on his damp fatigue jacket and continued to move.

After twenty minutes, the firing at the wall finally faded into sporadic shots, and Bolan reached the far end of the gully. He couldn't move any farther without exposing himself to the men at the wall. He rose slowly and stared down. Three of the enemy soldiers were exposed, if he wanted to take the shots, but he decided not to. He'd let them think he was still at the other end of the gully.

He decided to ignore the men at the wall, who wouldn't be moving until after dark. They had their own sniper out there and were under no pressure to get out. They could afford to wait. Bolan turned his scope on the tree lines behind them, searching for the Rifleman.

For nearly twenty minutes he saw no sign of the enemy. There were flashes of motion in the jungle twelve hundred meters away, but each time it turned out to be a bird taking flight or a monkey swinging through the upper branches of a tree. Each time Bolan almost fired, his finger caressing the trigger, and each time he hesitated, hoping for a better shot.

The setting sun suddenly became his ally. He knew that the Rifleman had had enough time to get into a position where Bolan might be vulnerable. He also knew the man hadn't spotted him yet because he hadn't fired. At the moment it was a stalemate, each man waiting for the other to break cover.

It was a strange situation. The men at the mud wall meant nothing now. They were the bait—Bolan's bait to draw out the Rifleman and the Rifleman's bait to draw him out. The Rifleman, now that he was on the scene, would have to protect them because to do less would undermine his support the next time he formed a security squad.

Bolan turned his attention to the squad again. He could still see two men; the third had moved off somewhere else. The wounded soldier no longer lay in the corner of the rice paddy. During Bolan's crawl, the man had either gotten out of there or someone had dragged him to safety.

It was getting darker by the minute. Anyone firing now would have his position marked by a muzzle-flash that would look like a beacon. No longer was the sun bright enough to wash it out.

Bolan surveyed his own position. He was exposed on the right but doubted the enemy was there. That was the direction he'd come from, and he would have seen anyone dropping into that spot. There was a slight rocky outcropping to the left, which would protect him if he moved closer. He rolled onto his back and searched the hill behind him. There was no cover there. The Rifleman couldn't be hidden up there unless he had dug a spider hole before the day had started. But then he wouldn't be in a position to spot Bolan.

Again all the advantages seemed to be his. Pick off the two soldiers he had spotted, and then wait for the Rifleman to shoot back. Maybe that would give him the shot he needed. If not, wait for dark and then crawl up the hill, calling artillery in to blast the men at the wall.

He waited a moment longer, giving the night a chance to become a little darker. Then, as the last light faded, Bolan put his sights on one of the men he could still see. He fired one round, and the man stood straight up as if stung in the butt by a bee. He held his rifle out in front of him and took one step. As he collapsed into the dirt, the few men who still lived opened fire again, but they were shooting at the spot where Bolan had been.

Bolan aimed at the second man but didn't fire. Something told him the timing was wrong. Instead of shooting, he withdrew, and then retreated so that he was behind the rocky outcropping. He waited there, then dived to the left, rolling onto his back.

The single shot came from a long distance. There was a single wink of light, but too far away for it to do Bolan any good. The bullet passed over him, striking the rock and whining off into the night. He thought he knew where the Rifleman was hidden, but the knowledge was worthless. Bolan would never be able to spot him in the scope now that it was night.

Rather than give the enemy a chance to sneak up on him, Bolan began to crawl up the hill. He kept his movements slow and regular, but now that it was night it would be almost impossible for the enemy to see him. Keeping his rifle in his hands, he crawled on his elbows, knees and feet. He tried to avoid making noise, all the while listening for the enemy coming after him.

The shooting from the wall tapered off, then stopped altogether. Bolan wished they would keep it up because it told him where they were. Besides, none of the rounds were coming close to him. The noise helped cover any sound he might make.

Then he was at the top of the hill, lying there with the valley spread out on one side and the jungle on the other. Protection was only a hundred meters away, a quick sprint if he had to run. Once inside the bush, the NVA wouldn't have much chance of finding him, and by morning he would be within a few meters of the camp. When the sun was up again, he could walk straight into camp.

He turned and looked back. The valley was spread out in front of him like a dirty gray blanket. The mud wall was a black slash, and the hootches were black boxes. He could see little through the scope. The enemy soldiers weren't visible.

Of course he could always call for illumination. Put a couple of flares up over the valley and shoot at anything moving down there. But that no longer seemed to be the smart thing to do. While he did that, the VC and NVA could be filtering a company or a battalion in with the mission of finding him. He couldn't evade that many people.

For a moment he considered firing a single round to see what would happen, but decided that would only mark his new position. It was too dark for the Rifleman to return his fire. It was time to get out.

He made his way over the top of the ridge and began to work his way to the trees, listening for sounds of pursuit. He kept moving slowly, taking nearly an hour to reach the jungle. In that time he heard one soft call in Vietnamese, but didn't know if it was the enemy giving orders or a farmer trying to find his wife. The sound wasn't repeated and had come from a long way away.

When he reached the trees, he stopped and listened. The last thing he wanted to do was to stand up inside the bush and realize he had crawled into a trap. He lay there, trying to will himself to relax, giving the enemy a chance to grow impatient. Of course, if the Rifleman was there, he would have the patience to wait until Bolan moved, knowing that he would have him cold at daylight. Regular soldiers might give themselves away, but not the Rifleman.

But there were no indications that anyone was lying in wait. Bolan slipped into the trees, got to his feet and searched the jungle around him. There was the quiet buzzing of mosquitoes and stinging flies. Tiny claws scraped on the bark of the hardwoods and rattled the leaves. The night birds called to one another, but there was no evidence of humans.

The warrior began to work his way through the jungle, moving slowly and carefully. He kept his eyes roaming and his ears cocked, but didn't run into the enemy. They seemed to have pulled back, fleeing from the American camp that was Bolan's haven.

He moved steadily for a couple of hours, his muscles aching from the strain. First it had been the dash through the jungle, trying to leapfrog ahead of the enemy, then lying nearly motionless for hours and finally moving again. But this time he had to be careful, avoiding anything that made noise. It was a forced pace that didn't allow him to move naturally. It made his legs ache, the muscles stretch. But he had to maintain his pace.

Even with the sun gone, the heat and humidity of the jungle was trapped in the thick vegetation. Rain, from a couple of days earlier, dripped through the thick canopy slowly, filtering toward the ground, giving the trees, bushes and ferns a slimy wet feel that soaked his uniform as he brushed by.

Two hours later he crouched on one knee to rest. He felt the soft rotting soil under him and felt the moisture seeping through. He kept his head and eyes moving, searching for the enemy because he didn't dare relax completely. He had been awake for nearly three days, and if he sat down, his back to a tree, he would be asleep in moments. Tomorrow, when he reached the camp, he could shower and then lie on his cot, but now he had to stay awake, stay alert, or he would die.

When his breathing returned to normal, he was up and moving. Overhead were the sounds of jets and helicopters searching for enemy troop movements. Charlie operated under the cover of darkness, and the American units with the highest kill counts operated at night when Charlie was out. Others, on search-and-destroy missions during the day, kept the enemy from resting then. It was a well-coordinated effort that drove the enemy day and night with some success. Coupled with the sniper program, they were slowly pushing the enemy from the region.

It was close to dawn when Bolan arrived at the edge of the jungle near his camp. Again he crouched, resting, letting the sun come up so that the trigger-happy guards on the perimeter wouldn't open fire when he showed himself. At night they shot at everything that moved, but in the daylight they tended to identify the target before they killed it.

As the sun rose, the jungle burst into activity. Monkeys suddenly started shrieking and leaping through the treetops. Birds that had been sleeping opened their wings and took off, squawking. Insects and lizards awoke, and a few spiders that had been hunting in the dark scrambled into hiding, afraid of the sun.

When Bolan saw activity in the camp, he popped a smoke to draw attention to himself. As the smoke billowed into a swirling cloud, caught in the early-morning breeze, he stepped from the jungle, holding his rifle over his head. Then, slowly, he started forward, aware that half a dozen machine guns were trained on him. At the first strand of wire he relaxed slightly and lowered his weapon. The men in the bunkers should have identified him as an American by now. He worked his way through the gaps until he reached the gate where two officers waited for him, hands on their hips.

"Well?" one said impatiently.

"Got a few of them," Bolan reported, "but not the Rifleman. Got some members of his security team. It had to be him out there, but I didn't get him."

"Okay. Take care of your weapon, then get yourself cleaned up and get some chow. I'll want a brief verbal report just as soon as you've finished that, and then you can get some sleep."

"Yes, sir."

"Oh, by the way. You now have a price on your head. G-2 picked up some leaflets yesterday offering the equivalent of nearly ten thousand dollars for you."

Bolan couldn't help grinning. He was dog-tired, dirty and hungry, but that was good news. It meant he was hurting the VC and NVA. If they bothered putting out a bounty, it was normally just a couple of hundred dollars at the most, maybe the equivalent of a year's pay. To offer ten thousand dollars, which was more than some Vietnamese would earn in a decade, meant they wanted him badly.

The officer grinned back. "If you keep giving me grief, I might try to collect it myself."

"You can try, sir," Bolan said. He wasn't joking.

7

Rachel Jamison stood just inside the front door, peeking through the small window as David Lee McDonald drove off with a squeal of smoking tires. She knew he had to be frustrated—he'd spent the night staring at her body, trying to see up her dress and down her blouse, touching her intimately at every opportunity, and then had had to leave without much more than a good-night kiss. Jamison shuddered as she remembered his pudgy wet lips pressing against hers as he'd tried to force his tongue into her mouth.

She had endured his hands on her body, but when he had managed to put one hand up her dress, she had gently pushed him away. "My mother might see," she'd told him.

McDonald had taken a step back. "Shouldn't you have a place of your own by now?"

"No. I must take care of my mother. She is so old and alone. She needs me. Please don't be angry with me."

"I'm not angry," he'd replied. "Frustrated as hell, but not angry."

"Maybe next time we can go to your place for a while, but tonight I must attend to Mother."

"All right," McDonald had said.

He'd left then, and she'd watched him drive away, wondering if she should wash her mouth out. As soon as his taillights disappeared around the corner, she was out the door again, hurrying down the street and up the walk to another house. The front door opened before she reached it.

"Well?" a male voice asked when the door had been shut securely behind her.

Jamison stumbled into the front room and collapsed into a chair. A pool of light illuminated one corner, leaving the majority of the room in shadows, hiding it from her. She could barely make out the young man sitting on the old couch, a slender, dark man with jet-black hair and almond-shaped eyes.

"Give me a minute," she said "I have to have a minute to think about this."

The man leaned forward, elbows on his knees, hands clasped under his chin. "You didn't have to make love with him tonight, did you?"

"Not tonight." She grinned. "He was in bad shape when he left me, though. He was so frustrated that he was shaking. Next time he'll be falling all over himself to tell me everything he can."

"Good. Now what did you get?"

"There wasn't much. He's not terribly bothered by the disappearance of his man in Vietnam. He assumes some kind of natural accident killed or injured him and seems to have rejected the idea that the man might have been discovered. When I asked if someone else would follow, he said no one had been chosen to do so, but I think someone will."

"Why?"

She shrugged. "Because the Americans can never leave well enough alone. They don't have the patience to wait for the results. They have to keep picking at something until they get themselves into real trouble."

"Anything else?"

"Are we interested in information from Central America?"

"I don't think so. There are others following those leads. All we want to know is what's happening in our own section of the world."

"All right, then. That's all. I had to be careful because he began questioning my interest in all this." She held up a hand to keep him from speaking. "Don't worry. I was able to cover it so that he isn't suspicious."

The man emerged from the darkness to stand near her. He stared down at her legs, making her feel uncomfortable. She wanted to tug at the hem of her short skirt but didn't want to draw attention to it as she had when McDonald had been with her.

The man knelt in front of her and slipped forward, forcing her knees apart with his hips. He touched the soft skin of her inner thighs and let the fingers of both hands roam higher as he held her legs against him.

His lips brushed hers, then touched the point of her chin and her throat, working lower. For a moment she suffered his kiss, then sat back in her chair, moving away from him, trying to hold him off.

"Please. After the night with *him*, I don't feel in the mood."

The man pushed his hand higher until it touched the silk of her panties. He rubbed her with his thumb, but when she failed to respond he stood up.

"You just remember what your job is."

"I don't think that I could ever forget." She got to her feet, smoothed her skirt and walked to the door. Someday it would all be over, she told herself, but she was afraid it wouldn't be soon enough.

WHEN COLONEL MOORE FINISHED briefing Bolan, he left the conference room, saying only that transportation had been arranged and the flight would leave in about two hours.

Warringer stood up. "That gives us just enough time to get to the airport and get you checked through the ticket counter."

"Great." Bolan looked at the material Moore had left—a map of Vietnam and two aerial photographs that showed virtually nothing. Everything else had been classified secret so that Moore was obliged to take it with him and lock it back in a safe where it wouldn't do anyone any good. Typical of the government.

As he moved toward the door, Bolan said, "I had hoped to get a chance to see the Special Forces museum and the monument before we had to leave."

Warringer nodded sympathetically. "Not really enough time now, but we can drive by there if you like. You can take a quick look around. It won't delay us that long."

"No, I guess we'd better not. I want to take the time necessary to study it closely, see it in detail, take the time to reflect on what has happened to us all. It's something I've promised myself I would do someday, but not if I've got to worry about an airplane.''

"I understand."

They left the building and stepped into the blazing heat and oppressive humidity of North Carolina. In the time it took them to reach the car, their clothes were marked with patches of perspiration.

"The thing I never get used to," Warringer said, "is the damned climate here. It's so hot and humid that I think it's worst than the tropics."

"No, there's nothing worse than Vietnam. At least here they're not shooting at you."

Warringer unlocked the driver's door and stood back to let the oven heat of the car's interior boil out. Over the roof he said, "They shoot at us in Fayetteville."

"But not with heavy artillery. No mortars or rockets or cannons."

"No, just a Saturday Night Special that's as liable to blow up in the hand as it is to shoot." Warringer ducked inside, unlocked Bolan's door, then reappeared. "Let's give the breeze a chance to cool it off in there."

Bolan stood for a moment, looking at the fort. It had been a long time since he'd been there in training. First to Benning for jump school, then back to Bragg for the unconventional warfare. Everything had seemed so much easier in those days. The real enemy was in Vietnam, and you didn't have to worry about him until you got there. The few times he'd run into the locals in Fayetteville it hadn't been much of a fight. They'd fled when they'd realized he wasn't just another of the thousands of soldiers assigned to

Bragg. The clerks, typists, mechanics and cooks were easy marks for the prostitutes, muggers and thieves. Soldiers got themselves robbed all the time. Bolan often wondered why the military didn't just clean things up. The town already hated them, anyway.

"I think it's cool enough." Warringer slid behind the wheel and put the key into the ignition to start the engine. He turned the air conditioner up high and pointed the vents at the steering wheel. Then, gingerly, he extended a cautious finger to see if it had cooled at all.

Bolan climbed into the other side and ignored the heat. He found himself drifting automatically into the mind-set he'd used in Vietnam. The heat wasn't all that bad if you didn't think about it. The humidity made it worse, but it was still better than the dank, dark coolness of a grave. That was an experience he wasn't quite ready for.

Warringer pulled his door closed and slipped the car into reverse. He backed up and pulled out of the slot, heading toward Smoke Bomb Hill. Hundreds of soldiers were training—men in combat boots, T-shirts and fatigue pants jogging along the road; others in gym clothes doing calisthenics; men practicing close-order drill; still others sitting in the shade of the evergreens drinking beer and applauding loudly. Like everywhere else, there was a handful of women scattered among all the men, training as they were.

They drove through the Special Forces areas. Buildings from the Second World War were prominent, but other, newer structures of white cinder block stood baking in the sun. The post had changed, and yet somehow it had remained the same.

They proceeded through the main gate and followed Bragg Boulevard into Fayetteville, which was a part of the journey Bolan would have avoided if the choice had been his. It was a dirty, miserable place that owed its existence to Fort Bragg, though the people of the town would never accept that as fact. They would argue the point long and hard.

It took them forty minutes to reach the civilian airport, which wasn't in Fayetteville, but in one of the outlying communities. From there Bolan would catch a flight to Atlanta, which was fast becoming a hub for air traffic throughout the South. Nearly every flight into the region landed in Atlanta, and a traveler could catch a connecting flight to anywhere in the world.

In the parking lot of the small airport, Bolan got out and retrieved his suitcase from the back seat of the car. He turned to Warringer. "You don't have to come in. I can find my way to the gate and the airplane."

The sergeant slipped the car into neutral, then stared up at the Executioner. "I was told to see you off. Those were my orders. Not to take you to the airport and leave you, but to see you off."

"Well, it's not necessary. Take the rest of the afternoon off. Go on home and drink a beer."

"Okay, thanks. And good luck to you."

Bolan gave him a thumbs-up and headed into the terminal building. The area between the double doors was boiling hot, but once he entered the terminal proper it was much cooler. Dozens of military men were milling about, waiting for flights out. There were only a few women, some with sadness etched into their faces because their men were leaving for short tours.

Others were happy because they were getting out permanently.

Bolan made his way to the ticket counter and waited in the short line. When it was his turn to be served, he checked his bag, then surveyed the crowd behind him, searching for a familiar face. He was looking for someone who didn't belong in the terminal, someone who was out of place. There was no reason to suspect he was being followed, but then there was no reason to take unnecessary chances. Certain rules had applied in Vietnam: never use trails, never use a machete and never break the branches of bushes. Any sign you left behind could be read by the enemy, and that could get you killed.

With his baggage checked, he stopped by the newsstand to buy a paper, then moved to the gate and sat down, out of reach of the sun burning through the windows, and watched the people circulate. He didn't suspect trouble, but he knew he couldn't be too careful. A little care could prevent trouble once he started the mission.

When his flight was announced, he and the other passengers boarded the commuter plane. Bolan relaxed once he was in the cabin, which contained a single row of seats lining either side of the fuselage. He had half expected Moore to send someone to watch him, although he didn't know why. Maybe it was just a mistrust of the military mind, reborn after being brought to Bragg for no good reason.

As the plane lifted off, Bolan's sense of uneasiness evaporated quickly so that he was ready when the flight attendant offered him something to drink. Once he had been served, he settled back to enjoy the rest of the flight to Atlanta. In just a few hours he would find it difficult to grab a chance to relax.

IN HIS HOOTCH Diem relaxed over a cold glass of wine. Normally he would have disdained such a bourgeois drink, but tonight he needed it badly, needed something to calm his nerves because some of the answers given to him by Ryan were frightening.

Maybe frightening wasn't the right word. Disturbing. That was it. Diem didn't like the idea that the Americans were sending agents into his country to spy. The last time the Americans had attempted that, it had escalated into a full-blown war that had killed hundreds of thousands of his countrymen. First a trickle, then advisers and finally combat soldiers. The cycle seemed to be starting again, and Diem didn't want to fight another war.

And then, as he thought about it, maybe he did. Again his mind turned to the times when he had been a soldier with more important duties. Not a jailer for old men who could barely stand, but a real soldier.

He stood up and looked at one of the pictures hanging on the wall, a black-and-white photo of him, holding his Mosin-Nagant, barrel pointed upward and butt snugged against his hip in a parody of the old white hunter pictures from Africa. Next to him was a young man, frozen in time, holding an AK-47. The man would never get any older because he had died shortly after the picture had been taken. An American sniper had killed him. Shot him in the back.

Diem stepped to the door and looked into the blackness of the Vietnamese early morning. There was almost no sound now. The traffic from the highway had ceased to move, and there were no aircraft overhead. The only sound was the hum of the generator, which ran all night to provide a small amount of electricity to the searchlights on the perimeter. They had to make sure the prisoners didn't try to escape, though the only place for them to go was the inhospitable jungle.

One of the guards spotted Diem and marched across the open ground to meet him. "Yes, Comrade?"

"I don't wish to be disturbed now. If anything happens, report to Comrade Minh. He'll answer your questions. Have someone wake me at nine if I don't appear before then."

"Yes, Comrade."

"How is the American doing?"

The guard shrugged. "He's lying on the floor, his arms around his belly, singing softly to himself. I don't know what he could be singing about."

"It's an American aberration. They laugh at danger and sing when in pain. Even when they shake with fear, they laugh and sing. I don't understand them, either."

Diem returned to his office and picked up his wineglass. He was apprehensive about something, but he couldn't put his finger on it. He found himself drawn to the pictures, and he studied each in turn carefully, moving down the row like a patron in an art museum, remembering the men he had fought with during the war against the American imperialists. These were men who had died in that war.

At the far end of the wall was a wanted poster, a line drawing of an American who had been a real threat to them. It was a good likeness of the man, one of the few Americans who had done real harm. Oh, there had been rewards for helicopter pilots and LRRPs, but this was a man who had commanded the highest of prices. Whoever killed him would have become a national hero, reaping rewards and honors at the highest level, and many men died trying to accomplish the feat.

Diem sat behind his desk and poured another glass of wine, lifted it to his lips and sipped it. Maybe the thing to do was to get drunk. A final binge. He hadn't allowed himself the privilege since the Americans had left. When he was fighting the war, he had to drink; now there was almost no reason for it.

Except that he had an American who had just arrived in Vietnam, a spy, and he didn't know what that meant.

He lifted his glass in a toast to the men who had died fighting the Americans, and took a deep drink. He thought about his friend, Tuy, who had helped him hunt the Americans for two months, thought about that last mission when Tuy died and Diem swore that he would kill the American who had shot him. The American who commanded the huge reward.

8

As a sniper, Diem had an advantage denied the Americans. They had to sneak into the area where they would work. Diem was already there. Most of the time the Americans barricaded themselves behind barbed wire and sandbags, hiding from the Vietnamese people. Diem was among them. He didn't have to go out in search of the enemy. He could lie quietly and wait for the enemy to come to him.

Both Diem and Tuy had worked their way to the top of a ridgeline, using the cover of darkness. Then they had disappeared into the ground through a spider hole. The trapdoor, concealed from the air, opened into a tunnel system that honeycombed that part of the valley and ridgeline. None of the tunnels were deep; most were barely five feet below the surface. Traveling through the system was difficult because the tunnels were only shoulder width, but the Americans had yet to stumble onto the network, and if they did, they wouldn't be able to get into it.

After they had eaten their morning meal of cold rice and fish heads, they made their way to one of the spider holes. Tuy climbed out, using the elephant grass to conceal his movements. He lay behind a rotting log, watching the valley floor, waiting for the first of the

Americans. He used a pair of U.S. Navy 7x50s, stolen during a raid at Nha Be.

While Diem sat in the spider hole, the cover closed, Tuy, sweating in the morning sun, studied the ground below him. At one point a flight of American helicopters flew over, filling the air with the sound of their rotors and the whine of their turbines. But that didn't bother Tuy. He knew if he lay still no one would see him. The Americans in the air, with a destination in mind, paid no attention to what was on the ground below them.

When the choppers had disappeared to the south, he turned his attention to the valley. Tuy finally saw movement near the tree line that protected a small river. He concentrated on that area and picked up a single man walking just inside the trees. As he watched, the man stopped, crouched then waved to someone concealed behind him. He was joined by another man who reached down and was handed something. Although Tuy couldn't see the handset in the distance, he knew that an officer had just been given the radio handset.

For a moment nothing happened, then more men appeared in the trees. They spread out and came forward, stepping into the morning sun. Unlike some soldiers, these men weren't afraid to walk in the water of the rice paddies. They avoided dikes, stepping on the plants. The platoon moved slowly, as if it were going through the motions but expected to find nothing. They were complacent soldiers.

"I have targets," Tuy hissed.

Diem popped up then, slipping from the spider hole slowly so that there wouldn't be a flash of movement to draw the enemy's attention. He crawled closer and peeked over the rotting log. Through a haze created by the tops of the blowing grass, he could see the Americans on line, sweeping toward a solitary farmer's hootch.

Diem raised his rifle and set the barrel on the log, using that for his bench rest. He peered through the scope, drawing a bead on the man who was obviously the officer. The target didn't wear a helmet like the rest of the Americans. Instead, he sported a baseball cap. He stopped and pointed, as if shouting orders, and stayed close to the man with the radio, apparent by the antenna above his head.

In many armies the death of the officer in charge was a real blow. He knew the mission and the job, and if he died, the men wouldn't know what to do because no one else would have been briefed. In the American army, if the man in command died, the next in line took over. Anyone—down to the lowest private in the lowest squad—could take over. In some units this procedure operated better than in others.

But Diem didn't care. The death of the officer in charge would slow them down. And if someone took over, trying to move them, Diem would kill him, too. That would take the starch out of their sails.

He nodded to the right. "Range?"

"Seven hundred meters."

Diem checked his scope and took careful aim at the officer. He could see the man clearly—a skinny American with a deep tan who had been in Vietnam a long time. The tan and the faded material of his fatigues were dead giveaways. And yet he was making mistakes the rawest recruit would make during his first days in Vietnam and who, if he survived, would learn from them. Diem wondered if the officer had spent his time in his camp, rarely venturing into the field.

As the Americans swept toward him, Diem checked the wind. The breeze was light, but it was blowing across his field of fire, which complicated the problem slightly. The shot would be more difficult than it would be if the wind was behind him.

The Americans advanced to the edge of the rice paddies and spread out, some soldiers sitting on the dry dirt of the dikes, resting. Perfect. Diem aimed carefully, made an adjustment to compensate for the wind, then caressed the trigger. The weapon fired, but none of the Americans reacted.

Then suddenly the officer grabbed his shoulder and tumbled into the water. One man leaped at him, snagged his shoulder harness and dragged him out of the paddy. The rest of the platoon scrambled for cover, but without the uncontrolled panic that sometimes set in with men running into one another in their attempts to hide. These men thought they knew where the shot had come from, and they leaped to the opposite side of the paddy dikes, hiding in the dirty water, waiting for a chance to return fire.

Not that it would do any good. Diem was high enough that he could see them spread out. Most were partially concealed, but there were plenty of targets. Now the question was whether to fire again, or wait for the helicopter that would be called in to pick up the wounded man. He might be able to pick off one of the pilots if he was patient.

"I have the radio operator spotted," Tuy whispered.

Again, a decision. Shoot the man and the radio, destroying the Americans' contact with their base, or wait to see if he could get a shot at the helicopter? And if he waited, the Americans might call in the gunships, which would hover over the whole area like angry bees waiting to strike.

Diem decided he could shoot another soldier without endangering himself. They were too far away. The sound of the shot would be lost in the echoes, and the muzzle-flash would be lost in the bright dazzle of the sun.

He targeted the man he thought was in command now that the platoon leader was down, and aimed again, waiting for the man to stop moving before he began to squeeze the trigger. But the American leaped over a dike and disappeared for a moment. Diem didn't let that bother him because he knew the man hadn't vanished. He would soon stand or move, and Diem would be right there to zero in on him.

Patience—it was one thing the Americans didn't understand. They were always in a hurry. Never walk when you can run. Never drive at twenty when you can do fifty. Always in a hurry. Hurry to find the enemy. Hurry to kill them. Hurry to end the war. The Americans would lose because they didn't understand patience. They didn't understand lying in the grass for days on end, waiting for the right target to come along, such as a platoon of soldiers that could be pinned down easily and taken out one by one.

The new leader stood up again and moved along the line. Already the Americans were becoming impatient, fidgeting in the paddy, aiming their rifles at nothing, probably demanding permission to shoot at the hootch, although it was obvious the shot hadn't come from there.

Diem watched the leader, and when the man finished his rounds, he fired. The bullet struck the soldier low in the back, punching him over a dike and into the water. His arms flailed, as though he were trying to swim, but instead he dragged himself out of the water and onto the dike. Diem thought about getting off another shot and killing him, but the dead had no value. Two wounded soldiers would bring the chopper faster.

There was a rattling of small-arms fire, and bullets snapped over Diem's head. The Americans had spotted the lair, but that didn't faze Diem. He touched Tuy on the shoulder and nodded at the spider hole. They would disappear into the ground and resurface a hundred, two hundred meters away, and take a few more shots. Let the Americans think the hillside was alive with enemy soldiers. Let them call in artillery and air strikes, maybe a company or two. Let them use hundreds of men and spend hundreds of thousands of dollars trying to kill the yellow hordes in the hills. He and Tuy would use the tunnels to crawl to safety, laughing at the Americans' antics.

The gunfire tapered off, and the sniper looked at the scene below him. Nothing had changed. Several soldiers crowded around the wounded men, trying to save their lives.

The two Vietnamese crawled over and dropped into the spider hole, working their way along the tunnels. They had to be careful, avoiding the booby traps and false tunnels that had been dug to kill and injure anyone small enough and foolish enough to follow.

The dank odor of the dirt filled their nostrils as they worked their way along the system. It was hard to see in the dim light after the brightness of the morning sun. But the coolness was a relief from the punishing heat.

They eased downward into a chamber that widened slightly. Diem sat up, resting against the packed earth of the tunnel wall. He leaned his head back and closed his eyes, breathing slowly. It was the first opportunity he'd had to relax since he'd crawled into the predawn mist.

Tuy reached over and touched his knee. Diem opened his eyes and the other man nodded down the tunnel. It was time to get moving again. The sniper led the way, entering another of the narrow tunnels, crawling on his elbows, knees and the sides of his feet. He pulled a trapdoor, opening it carefully. A sharp tug or jerk would have armed a grenade set to detonate at the top of the tunnel, throwing shrapnel in every direction.

They eventually came to another of the spider holes that led to the surface. Diem was up first, carefully lifting the door, searching the surrounding countryside for signs of the enemy. But the Americans hadn't moved from the rice paddies where they tended their wounded.

The two NVA were lower on the hill, so they didn't have the view of the Americans that they'd had earlier. But that didn't matter much. Diem could still see some of the soldiers as they crawled around trying to find adequate cover behind the short dikes, hoping that the sniper had fled.

"You want the next shot?" Diem asked.

Tuy glanced at his friend. Rarely were they in a position where they could trade shots. Normally Tuy was the spotter, using binoculars to identify the targets while Diem picked them off. After one or two shots, they were off and running, trying to avoid the Americans.

Tuy nodded.

"Only one, though. We want that chopper to come in so that we can shoot the pilots."

"I understand."

Diem handed over the rifle, taking the Kalashnikov in return. He checked the safety and then waited as Tuy stretched out and wrapped the sling of the sniper rifle around his arm. He steadied his arm but didn't try to move a log or rock in front of him to use as a bench rest. Now that the Americans knew they were on the hill somewhere, he didn't want any unnecessary movement giving away their exact position. Besides, the targets weren't moving much, and they weren't more than five hundred meters away. It was a shot that could be made with a rifle with fixed sights and no scope if the triggerman was fairly steady.

With the scope, Tuy searched the faces of the men below him, selecting the one who would soon die. He didn't want to kill a regular infantry soldier, because Tuy felt an affinity for them—he was regular infantry himself. A man with no rank, told what to do and how to do it by a variety of superiors, from the corporal at their base camp right up to the majors and colonels who directed the lives of all the men around them. Tuy wanted a target of significance.

He found a man who had black smudges sewn to the collar of his jungle fatigues, a man who moved among the others, looking as if he were giving orders. The target didn't wear a heavy pack like the other men and didn't carry a rifle. He wore a pistol on his hip, and to Tuy that meant he was an officer.

"I'm going to shoot now," Tuy warned.

Diem brought the binoculars to his eyes and checked the surrounding countryside. "It's clear. Take him when you're ready."

Tuy took a deep breath, then exhaled. With the sight post on his target, he squeezed the trigger. The round exploded from the rifle, the butt slamming into his shoulder. He kept the scope focused on his target and clearly saw the bullet strike. It was high, hitting the enemy in the shoulder in a splash of crimson. The man simply slumped to the ground as others reached for him.

"Good!" Diem congratulated him. "Beautiful shot. Another wounded man. Now we must lie low."

There was a delayed reaction from the men in the paddies. Gunfire rippled from below, single shots, then one sustained burst from an M-60 machine gun. But all of it was directed to a spot higher on the hill, where Diem and Tuy had struck first. The dirt churned under the withering fire, fountains of dust exploding into the bright sky.

Seconds later there was an ear-numbing rumbling overhead and a mushrooming explosion as black dirt erupted. A second round fell short of the first, and the whole side of the hill began to disintegrate. Someone below was directing artillery to Diem and Tuy's previous position.

Diem watched as the American artillerymen achieved a rhythm, dropping their rounds close to one another. The air was split with the explosion, the earth-shattering noise washing out all other sound. It would have been the perfect time for Diem to fire on the Americans, but he didn't want them to know he was still alive. Let them believe he and Tuy had died in the artillery barrage. Let them call in their helicopters.

As the last echoes of the artillery explosions faded into the distance, there was the drumming beat of rotor blades. Far to the northeast he saw sunlight flash on the windshield of the approaching chopper. Without a word, he took his Mosin-Nagant from Tuy as they switched roles again.

He crawled to the right now, where there was a large boulder to steady his aim. He wanted to make sure he had a good bench rest because it was hard to kill pilots. They sat in armored seats, wore chest protectors and hid behind the metal of instrument panels. His shot would have to be perfect.

Smoke billowed from the rice paddies, marking the landing site for the chopper. Two men ran to the left and threw themselves down as if providing flank security. Another crouched near the growing cloud of yellow smoke, his rifle held above his head, as if directing the chopper.

Diem was tempted to shoot the man, but knew that the second he did, the helicopter would break off the landing to wait until the LZ was secure. Patience, he told himself.

The chopper circled far to the west so that it came straight at him, changing from a gnat to a mosquito to a bird. Through the rifle's scope, he could make out the insignia painted on the nose, could see the hook hanging under the belly and make out the shapes of the pilots behind their Plexiglas windshields.

Let them land, he told himself. Shooting at a stationary target was easier than firing at a moving one. Let them come to him. Do it right.

He began the ritual of steadying himself. He took a deep breath and held it for an instant before exhaling. He was watching everything around him through his scope: the men in the rice paddies, their uniforms soaked and mud-smeared; the wounded men lined up like the dead, covered with blood and bandages; others running around on missions that made no sense; men hoping that the snipers had been killed by the artillery, but who were playing into Diem's hands.

The chopper was on short final, no more than thirty-five meters above the ground. The man in the smoke had stood, holding his rifle high over his head. In a moment they would get a real surprise. Diem saw the pilots clearly through his telescopic sight, and they were close enough that he could make out their faces.

Now was the time. Shoot the pilot and see if the helicopter would crash.

And then, over the pounding of the rotor blades and the scream of the turbine, came the sonic crack of a rifle bullet. It whipped by Diem's ear and ended with a wet, sickening slap. Tuy grunted and dropped facedown, blood spurting from the wound in his back and spraying Diem and the ground around them.

Without consciously thinking, Diem rolled to the right, twisting around so that he was up against the solid rock. He turned his rifle, eye to the scope, but couldn't spot his adversary. A second shot slammed into the rock inches from his head. Diem heard it strike and ricochet, felt the vibrations in the stone, but didn't move. He doubted the man would have missed if he'd had a clear shot. Diem had found the best protection available, instinctively.

He glanced at Tuy. The man hadn't moved. His back was covered with blood, and there was a spreading pool of crimson under him. The flies had already begun to gather.

The NVA turned his attention to the upper slopes of the hillside. There was a copse and a line of trees that dipped into the valley like the fat finger of a giant reaching over the crest. The elephant grass, about a meter tall, could hide the enemy's blind. Unless he fired again or moved, Diem had no hope of spotting him and then no hope of an eye for an eye—the American sniper had killed his closest friend.

Below him the helicopter was lifting off now. It turned and retreated, never coming near the hill. The men were up and moving, sweeping across the rice paddies quickly, trying to reach the cover at the base of the hill. Once there it would be difficult to shoot at them without exposing himself. And there was the enemy sniper somewhere above him. Diem had to get out, or he was going to die.

The expected course of action would be for him to try to reach the spider hole five meters away—except that it was on the other side of Tuy's body and as far away as Hanoi. The second he moved, the sniper would shoot him. Unless he did something unexpected.

He waited for a moment, letting everyone settle down a bit. Let the enemy sniper think that things had stopped. Then he would leap up, jump over the top of the rock and drop behind it. Twenty meters away there was another spider hole. If he timed it right, he might reach safety before anyone realized what he was up to.

He hated to leave Tuy's body, but that couldn't be helped. There was nothing on it that would tell the Americans anything. They would find his weapon, but no papers and no equipment. If they located the spider hole, they would drop a grenade down it in the mistaken belief that it would collapse part of the tunnel. The spider hole would be of no use later, but the tunnel system would remain intact.

Far in front of him, the Americans were beginning to sweep up the hill, coming for him. Diem counted silently to himself, put his hands under his body, as if he were about to do a push-up, and leaped to his feet. He dived over the rock and rolled close, but there was no shot from the American sniper and no shooting from the American infantrymen. It was possible that they hadn't seen him.

Hoping for the best, he began to crawl down the hill toward the spider hole. He used the grass to conceal himself, slipping through it cautiously, trying not to cause a ripple, hoping the light breeze would hide his movements. He kept the motion steady, not thinking about the American sniper, although he was sure the man was aiming at him. A spot at the base of his skull ached as he thought about the enemy's cross hairs centering on it. But he kept moving, never hesitating.

At the edge of the spider hole he stopped for a moment. He could have shot a couple of the Americans moving toward Tuy's body, but then it would have been impossible for him to get away. They would spot him, and with the cover available to them now, they could work their way close enough so that they could lob grenades at him. He didn't want to sacrifice himself unnecessarily because he had a score to settle. The man who had killed Tuy would have to die, and if Diem was killed now, he couldn't find and kill the man.

Without a thought, he lifted the trapdoor of the spider hole, certain that someone would see the movement. He slithered into the hole and pulled the door shut. The Americans would approach carefully, watching. It would take them a long time to reach the spot, and Diem would use the time to crawl along the tunnels, heading up the hill until he reached a portion that was under the trees. Once there, he could exit to make his escape, or he could rest through the heat of the afternoon while the Americans knocked themselves out trying to find him.

He crawled away, setting the booby traps behind him in case a brave man entered the spider hole. If someone did, he would be unable to travel very far before hitting the traps.

As Diem got clear, he remembered the sound of the bullet slamming into Tuy's body. He heard the quiet grunt over and over as his friend died, shot in the back by an American. Diem would kill him because he knew who had fired the shot. It could only have been one man. The man everyone called the Executioner.

DIEM FELT TIRED. His eyes burned and his head spun. It was the effect of the wine and the lack of sleep. And the memories of the Executioner. He'd stalked the man for a couple of years, never knowing if he was still in Vietnam or not. He'd even made plans to sneak into the United States to find him, but those plans had never been put into effect. Now they were a dream. Someday he would go to the United States and search out the Executioner, killing him for shooting Tuy in the back.

Diem felt the anger swell through him. Given half a chance, he would have killed the American. There was no doubt that he would have. He should have stayed on the hillside that day to make sure that he got the man, but at the time it had seemed more prudent to get out. Live to fight another day. He'd had the man in his sights more than once since then. He'd shot at him and been shot at by him.

The colonel touched his shoulder where the thick, ropelike scar blemished his skin. It was a bullet wound that ached as the weather changed, that ached all through the wet season and ached when the humidity was high. Another gift from the Executioner. The man's luck had been very good once, a long time ago, but that wouldn't save him. He would have grown soft in the years since he'd left Vietnam.

As he had done a dozen times, a hundred times, he took paper from his desk and began to write his letter of resignation. He would quit the army, leave Vietnam and make his way to the United States. It would be a simple thing for him to do. The Vietnamese government would grant him permission to travel to Bangkok, and from there he could fly to the United States. And the Americans were now proud of their Vietnam exploits. It would be a simple thing to find the sniper who was known as the Executioner. Diem could be on a plane home before anyone knew the man was dead.

In the morning, he decided, he would write his letter. Write it when he was sober and could phrase it properly so that he didn't insult anyone with it. All he had to do was wait until morning.

9

The flight to Atlanta was uneventful. Bolan caught the plane to Los Angeles, switched to the flight to Bangkok and then sat back to wait. It was almost like the flight to Vietnam so many years before, except that he wasn't surrounded by young men who were on their way to fight a war no one understood. Now there was a very good chance that everyone on the plane would survive their trip into Southeast Asia. On that first flight, there was a very good chance that half of them, maybe more, would not.

That plane had been a Boeing 707 with the seats crammed in close together. No shoulder room or leg-room, and the flight attendant wasn't allowed to serve alcohol, which was probably a good idea. The last thing they needed was a bunch of drunk soldiers who thought they would die soon anyway.

Bolan tried to remember what it had been like. There was something about the mood on the plane. Subdued. Even though the majority of the men were just nineteen or twenty, they weren't clowning around as most men that age would. Maybe it had been the long days waiting at the depot in San Francisco, or the bus ride to the Air Force base. Maybe everyone was worn out from parties and celebrations before they got to the plane as they tried to cram a lifetime into a few days of leave.

It was the unknown that bothered the men. Few soldiers had returned from Vietnam. There was no one to talk to about what it was like. Each man had seen the Saturday matinees where John Wayne had fought through hordes of Japanese, but few believed the movies. Besides, this was the war where you couldn't tell the good guys from the bad guys. The enemy could be your friend during the day and try to kill you at night. It was a great unknown. And that was what scared the hell out of everyone.

Bolan told himself that the training he'd received made him more aware of what it would be like. At Camp Mackall the instructors had been Vietnam vets, trying to tell the men what they would need to know to survive a year in the jungles of Vietnam. During the day, they made it sound like hell, but in the evenings they would sometimes talk about their nights in the bars of Saigon. Fights with the Navy, the Air Force and the Vietnamese. Women offering them everything they could think of, for a price. It didn't sound like the wars John Wayne fought on Saturday afternoon.

Now, in the Boeing 747, carrying three hundred people in relative comfort, it was difficult to revive that feeling of so long ago. The war hadn't been what Bolan had expected. He hadn't manned the outposts of freedom, with the Communist horde held at bay by grim determination and guts. It had been a war of attrition, searching through the jungle for an enemy who lived in trees. It had been a search for soldiers who had a dozen places to hide and who knew how to use them.

You could walk by a man, step on him and never realize it.

There were so many things that Hollywood conditioned recruits to expect, such as the explosions of grenades. In Hollywood movies giant explosions blew men into the air and killed them. In combat they were small bangs and puffs of smoke that could rip you apart with shrapnel. That was the killing danger of grenades. Not the concussion that Hollywood portrayed.

And people hit with bullets weren't blasted from their feet and thrown through the air. That did happen, but most of the time they collapsed into screaming heaps covered with blood. Or they began to flop around like a fish out of water. All things that Hollywood ignored.

He shook himself from the memories and forced himself to look out of the plane. The water under him sparkled and flashed in the afternoon sun. To the north the clouds of a mounting storm system swirled and boiled, and lightning flashed. Another great contrast to where he was.

Bolan leaned back against the headrest and closed his eyes. If someone had asked what he remembered about that first trip, he would have told them about the chaplain who had moved through the plane giving bad advice and telling the soldiers it would all be over before they knew it. To Bolan, that had meant they might all be dead in a week. The chaplain should have told the men they would be on their way home before they knew it. Even after all this time, he could still remember the man's words.

He couldn't remember anything about the flight attendants, although they must have served a meal or two. He must have eaten during the flight, but he didn't remember any food. There had been a movie, a simple-minded comedy, maybe selected because it was a comedy. And they all had had to fill out a customs declaration before they had landed, as if they could have possibly smuggled something into Vietnam to make the situation worse.

In the years since that first trip, he had forgotten a lot of the details. Maybe he'd spent most of the time wondering if he'd be able to survive that kind of warfare. Or maybe he'd spent it sleeping.

The flight attendant moved through the plane now, asking the passengers what they would like to eat. She took the orders—fish, beef or chicken—and returned to the front, a pretty woman with long blond hair and nearly perfect teeth. She had a smile for everyone and shrugged off the advances of a drunken male passenger with practiced grace.

Bolan looked at his watch and realized it would be about the middle of the day when they landed in Bangkok. With all the delays at airports and the changing of planes, the trip would take nearly twenty-four hours. Halfway around the world in a single day.

Again he turned his interest to the window, but now they had left the storm far to the rear. Bolan closed his eyes, figuring he could catch a little sleep while all the flavor was being microwaved out of his dinner.

McDONALD SAT IN HIS OFFICE reading the latest intelligence traffic, wishing instead that he was reading something that contained pictures. His mind wasn't on his work. It was on Rachel Jamison and her refusal to go home with him. That had left him in an agitated state, and he'd been unable to sleep when he reached his home. He'd needed relief, and the cold shower he'd suffered hadn't helped. Instead, he had lain awake, trying not to think about Rachel's soft skin, her round hips and how it felt as he... He sighed and made a greater effort to concentrate on the report.

The knock on the door brought an almost physical sense of relief. He quickly covered the classified documents, glanced at the safe to make sure nothing showed and yelled, "Come on in."

Lieutenant Commander William Weeks opened the door. A man of about fifty, he was short, thick and tanned and had close-cropped hair sprinkled with gray. His tailored uniform had been purchased cut-rate on a recent trip to Hong Kong, and it fit like a glove. The ribbons above his left breast pocket showed a tour in Vietnam, but the lack of combat awards suggested the trip had been less than successful.

He entered the tiny office, waving a telex like a banner. Without invitation, he slipped into the visitor's chair and stared at McDonald. "Got a question for you, David Lee."

McDonald rubbed his chin and realized he could have shaved closer that morning, but at the time he hadn't wanted the razor in his shaking hand near his throat longer than was strictly necessary. "And what's your question?"

"You heard anything more from that guy you sent into Vietnam?"

"Keep your voice down," McDonald warned. "It's not common knowledge around here." He stood and

Play "Action Poker" to see if you can get

- ◆ 4 hard-hitting, action-packed Gold Eagle novels just like the one you're reading — FREE
- ◆ PLUS a useful pocket knife — FREE

Peel off the card on the front of this brochure and stick it in the hand opposite. Find out how many gifts you can receive ABSOLUTELY FREE. They're yours to keep even if you never buy another Gold Eagle novel.

Then deal yourself in for more gut-chilling action at deep subscriber savings

Once you have read your free books, we're willing to bet you'll want more of those page-crackling, razor-edge stories. So we'll send you six brand new Gold Eagle books every other month to preview. (Two Mack Bolans and one each of Able Team, Phoenix Force, Vietnam: Ground Zero and SOBs.)

- ◆ Hot-off-the-press novels with the kind of no-holds — barred action you crave.
- ◆ Delivered right to your home.
- ◆ Months before they're available in stores.
- ◆ At hefty savings off the retail price.
- ◆ Always with the right to cancel and owe nothing.

You will pay only $2.49 for each book — 11% less than the retail price — plus 95¢ postage and handling per shipment.

Enjoy special subscriber privileges

- ◆ With every shipment you will receive AUTOMAG, our exciting newsletter FREE.
- ◆ Plus special books to preview free and buy at rock bottom discount.

CLAIM YOUR FREE GIFTS! MAIL THIS CARD TODAY.

BUSINESS REPLY CARD

First Class   Permit No. 717   Buffalo, NY

Postage will be paid by addressee

Gold Eagle Reader Service
901 Fuhrmann Blvd.
P.O. Box 1394
Buffalo, NY 14240-9963

NO POSTAGE
NECESSARY
IF MAILED
IN THE
UNITED STATES

moved to the door. Opening it, he made sure there was no one in the hallway. When he was certain there wasn't, he closed the door and locked it. "Now, what do you want to know?"

"You heard anything from that guy?"

"No. Nothing at all from him, and nothing from our sources in Vietnam. He's completely disappeared."

"That's what I thought." Weeks shook his head sadly. "You superspooks can't do anything right. That wasn't a job for a spook. It was a job for us."

"As you mentioned half a dozen times during the planning," McDonald said dryly.

"I told you that guy would get himself lost."

McDonald waved a hand dismissively. "Is there a point to this, or did you just come in here to gloat?"

"The point is that I've received information from the States that a replacement has been dispatched."

"What?"

Weeks glanced at the telex he held. "Word came this morning. Some guy has been sent to see if he can learn what happened to your man. He's operating independently and isn't going to check in here unless he wants help."

"I don't like this."

"What's not to like? Washington sends us somebody to determine the fate of your missing man. We're to stay out of it. If the guy fails, or maybe I should say, *when* the guy fails, the pressure is off here. Now it's their responsibility."

"Suppose he succeeds?"

Weeks shrugged. "You really think there's much chance of that? Hell, man, he's got to cross Cambodia or Kampuchea or whatever the hell they call it now, enter Vietnam and find out what happened to one man who entered that country without an itinerary. How's he going to succeed?''

McDonald rocked back in his chair and grinned. "Guess there isn't much chance of that, is there?''

"Of course not. And when he fails, then we don't look so bad. If he disappeared, it would be the best thing that could happen for us.''

For an instant McDonald wondered if they should help him disappear, then decided against it. The man had enough working against him. They didn't need to erect unnecessary roadblocks. Besides, the man couldn't do any damage to them, even if he got in and got out.

Weeks leaned forward, hands on his knees as he prepared to stand up. "Guy's due in sometime today, I think. Message was a little vague on that point.''

"We know who it is?''

"Nope. We've been given nothing on this one, since it's an operation run from the States. I was alerted in case the man shows to ask for something. I'm telling *you* because you've got an interest in this.''

"Thanks, Bill. I appreciate your letting me know. If you learn anything else, I'd like to hear it.''

Weeks stood up. "You'll be the second to know.''

When Weeks was gone, McDonald tried to figure out how this would affect his career. He'd run one operation and that had ended in failure. His head was on the block for suggesting the mission, and although he hadn't selected the man for the job, Ryan's failure would become his. Failure wasn't considered a good career move unless it could be proved that the failure was the responsibility of someone else. Ryan was the weak link in the chain. He hadn't been as good in the jungle as he had claimed. He couldn't slip through it like a ghost or a light breeze. He had done something or stepped on something or been picked up by the Vietnamese. It didn't matter what because he hadn't reported.

Again McDonald wondered if he should let something leak to compromise the new mission. A failure there would take some of the sting out of his own failure.

Still, McDonald didn't like that idea. Compromising a mission for his own career advancement was wrong even if he didn't know the man who was coming in. Even if the fate of the free world wasn't hanging in the balance. There was just no justifiable reason to compromise it. And there was the possibility that the mission would fail without his help. He could only hope for the worst.

With that decision made, his thoughts returned to Rachel. Without wanting to, he felt himself growing impatient with desire for her. The promise he'd made to himself the night before evaporated. He wanted to see her again, if only to take his mind off the government troubleshooter.

He reached out and picked up the phone, but hesitated before dialing. If he called her, he was being weak. He had to be strong; he had to take the lead, call the shots. Then he smiled, because she knew nothing of the promise he had made to himself.

He punched the button for an outside line and dialed. As he listened to the ringing on the other end, he thought of taking Rachel to his house for an after-

noon of fun and games. Maybe a quick lunch, or
maybe they would skip lunch and have an early sup-
per. He would decide that as he talked to her.

THE CAPTAIN ANNOUNCED their descent into Bangkok as he turned on the seat belt sign. The flight attendant swept through the cabin, making sure
everyone had complied with the captain's orders.

Bolan gave himself a mental shake, wondering why
he was so moody. Maybe it was this mission. Maybe
it was the thoughts that had been swirling around in
his head after the trip to Bragg. Memories had been
stirred up, memories that had been buried since he had
been called back to the World after his family had
died.

The World. That was something he hadn't thought
of in years. The GIs in Vietnam had called the United
States the World, as if there were no other place on the
planet. And for most of them, there wasn't. Who
wanted to stay in that tropical hell where people were
trying to kill you?

The descent began gradually. They left the bright
afternoon sun and slipped into a thick bank of clouds.
The captain told them to ignore the weather. It was
only a rainstorm that would quickly blow itself out
and it wouldn't keep them from landing. The plane
bounced once, twice, then took a long plunge. There
were squeals from some of the women, and a few
grunts of surprise from the men, but soon the descent
leveled off and the captain was back on the intercom,
telling them there would be a little turbulence until
they landed.

Finally they touched down, and the captain greased it in as if to make up for the rough approach. The engines roared as they slowed the plane, then the pressure against the seat belts abated and they were taxiing toward the terminal.

The rain hadn't stopped. It was a gray day, the dark clouds close to the ground, boiling with activity. Water streamed down the windows as they moved closer to the jetway.

People started to clog the aisle even before the plane came to a stop, waiting for someone to open the doors. Bolan however, waited patiently, staring out the window. In the distance he could just make out the city with its distinctive Oriental flavor. There were palm trees growing tall, and even if he hadn't known he was in Bangkok, he could have guessed he was somewhere in Southeast Asia.

As his fellow passengers began to file out, Bolan stood and slipped into the line. He followed the crowd up the jetway, catching a slight whiff of the tropics, just a bare trace of it lingering as the air-conditioning fought to drive it out. Bolan hesitated at the window, but now could see little more than the wet runways and ramp.

Customs was a snap, only because he had brought so little with him. In less than an hour he was walking through the terminal, wondering what his first move should be. The military genius who had arranged the trip had also gotten him reservations at a downtown hotel, but Bolan wasn't convinced he should stay there. Once he was out the door, the best move might be to divorce himself from a planned itinerary. He didn't know who might have received a copy of it. It would probably be prudent to find his own accommodations.

He left the terminal and went out into the hot, humid air, which had a texture to it, a smell to it, that reminded him of Vietnam. Even the traffic flowing around him—the bicycles ridden by people drenched in the rain, the motor scooters and the Hondas, the few cars painted in every color under the rainbow. It was almost like stepping off the plane in Saigon, and he had a sudden assault of everything bad about Saigon.

For an instant he stood there, letting the warm, wet air wash over him. In seconds his clothes were damp from the fine mist carried by the hot wind. He was reminded of the day he'd gotten off the plane in Vietnam, a career soldier who hadn't fully realized what this particular war was about. Like the hundred or so other men, he had been herded into a hangar where he'd been told he was in Vietnam, and that what he would experience here would have nothing to do with the Saturday afternoon matinees he and the rest of the new men had seen in the World. This was war as it really was, and although no one was shooting at them for the moment, someone would begin soon enough.

The scene: tired, frightened men in sweat-stained uniforms sitting on metal folding chairs in front of an easel with a map of Vietnam on it. Huge fans stood on the floor, trying to stir up a breeze that did little to ease the heat and humidity. Jet aircraft roared into the sky, almost drowning the popping of rotor blades—sounds that would be around during most of the coming year.

But then the scene dissolved quickly as a car pulled up and the driver honked on the horn. He leaned across the front seat and rolled down the window. "You want ride?"

Bolan glanced to the rear and then decided to get in. He opened the door, tossed in his bag and slid across the seat.

The driver turned, his arm resting on the back of the seat. "Where you go?"

"Downtown. Need to find a hotel."

"You no got reservation?"

"Nope. I'm here on a whim. Just felt like coming to Bangkok to see how it looks."

"You want American hotel? Just like you have at home? Or you want local color?"

Bolan glanced in the rearview mirror and saw that the driver was examining him closely. It might have been idle curiosity, and Bolan wondered if he was becoming paranoid. He couldn't have been picked up so quickly, unless there was a leak, and as far as he knew, no one in Thailand had been told of his trip.

"Let's go for the local color," he said, figuring it would be easier to disappear from one of the locally run hotels. The American chains tended to keep too many records and watched their guests too closely.

Bolan decided to watch for a tail but doubted there would be one. He settled into the seat, and as the driver dropped the car into gear, he let his memories bubble to the surface.

Unlike many of the Special Forces men, he had been sent to Vietnam as an individual and not as part of an A-Detachment. That had opened the assignment process up so that he had landed a job that hadn't exactly been in the Special Forces syllabus. But then it had given him the opportunity to develop his own methods.

He sat up and glanced out the rear window of the cab, but there didn't seem to be anything of interest behind him. He had slipped into the country without the opposition, if there was one, identifying him.

With that determined, he returned to his thoughts of Vietnam, to the days of being shuffled from one command to another until he had ended up as part of a recon team operating from a small camp northwest of Saigon. Not a choice assignment, but better than living in the jungle all the time. It hadn't exactly been what he had expected, but then, if someone had asked, he couldn't have told them what he had anticipated, anyway. Vietnam was like that.

10

The tiny camp sat on the summit of a small hill that dominated the landscape for miles around. To the north and west was a sea of green that slowly turned into triple-canopy jungle. Far to the north was a sea of grass and reeds that marked a swamp where travel was confined to a few poorly maintained roads and paths where the enemy booby-trapped everything in sight. Closer in and to the east were rice paddies, hundreds of small paddies worked by dozens of farmers in black pajamas and coolie hats. Clumps of palm trees dotted the area and protected the farmers' hootches. There were a couple of small communities, a random selection of hootches, a small marketplace and a road or canal that connected them to the main thoroughfares that led to the big cities and eventually Saigon.

The camp itself was a collection of sandbagged bunkers and concertina wire like those the Americans had erected all over South Vietnam. The perimeter was guarded by machine guns, including a couple of the big Browning M-2 .50-caliber weapons. There were mortar pits to one side and a large bunker near the center, which was the TOC. The soldiers lived in bunkers made of green rubberized sandbags, but there were a few tents—a mess hall that was a large tent erected over a wooden frame, and a commo bunker identifiable by the radio antenna near it.

The chopper landed on a pad just outside the wire in a whirlwind of red dust and dried grass that obscured vision until it died down. Bolan leaped from the cargo compartment and let the crew chief hand him the equipment he'd drawn at Bien Hoa. As he shouldered his gear, the chopper lifted, creating a new dust storm. In seconds it was gone, leaving Bolan standing in a silence that was deafening, wondering if he was in the right place.

His confusion was short-lived. Two men left the perimeter. Both wore faded jungle fatigues that were now stained black by their sweat. Both carried M-14s and wore pistol belts complete with canteens and first-aid kits.

The bigger of the two stepped forward, his hand outstretched. "Welcome to Vietnam."

Bolan studied the landscape around him. "Thanks, anyway."

"I'm Sergeant Gibson and this is Sergeant Sommers."

"Bolan."

"Let's get you inside before the snipers decide you've lived long enough."

Sommers grabbed the duffel bag and shouldered it. "How'd you end up here?"

"You tell me. I thought I'd be assigned as a replacement to an A-Detachment."

Sommers turned and looked. "You're Special Forces?"

"That's right."

"Then someone really screwed up," Gibson said. "There aren't any green beanies on this hill. Nearest group is fifty klicks away."

Bolan shrugged. "Then I'll just have to get a transfer worked out."

Gibson slapped him on the shoulder. "Well, you can spend the night. We won't be able to get another chopper in here before tomorrow, anyway. Besides, I don't think Colonel Crawford will let you get away that easily."

Crawford was happy to see the new man, and less than enthusiastic when Bolan suggested a mistake had been made with his assignment to the camp. Crawford was a tall, heavy-set man who was balding rapidly. He was sunburned and had a permanent squint. When he met Bolan, he held out a beefy hand and nearly crushed Bolan's fingers.

After they sat down in the dank, dim bunker Crawford used for an office, the colonel informed him, "You're going to be here for a while. We've taken quite a few casualties in the past few weeks and we're shorthanded." The colonel leaned forward, his elbows resting on his shaky desk. "When we get back up to total strength, we'll get you back to the Special Forces, but right now I can use that extra training."

Bolan looked at his watch. "I've only been in Vietnam about thirty-six hours."

"But you've been in the Army a hell of a lot longer than most of the boys who arrive here."

That was true. Most soldiers had sixteen weeks of training, eight weeks in basic and then eight more in advanced individual training. Bolan, because of his Special Forces background, had accumulated a lot of specialized training in various jobs. Much of his recent instruction had been directed toward a tour in Vietnam.

Crawford stood up and moved to the battle map tacked to the thick planks of the bunker. It was covered with acetate and had the suspected locations of enemy troops circled in red grease pencil. He pointed to it and said, "We've been taking sniper fire for weeks. The guy is good. Maybe we could use some of your special skills to take him out."

"Excuse me, sir, but I've just—"

"Yeah, I know. You've only been here for thirty-six hours. But there's a war on. Sometimes we have to make sacrifices. You go catch some sleep and I'll have Sergeant Gibson find you permanent quarters and a weapon. You'll have to be ready to go out tomorrow."

There wasn't a thing Bolan could say. The colonel had given the orders, and the fact that most men got a week to acclimatize themselves with the country and to get over jet lag didn't seem to bother the man. Bolan would have to be ready to move out with a patrol in the morning. During his time in the Army, he'd learned one thing. The only possible response was "Yes, sir."

He was given a cot in the corner of a bunker. The interior smelled of dirt and sweat. There was a green haze around the cot—the mosquito netting. A naked bulb dangled from a bare wire in the center of the bunker, providing a little illumination.

Gibson dropped the duffel bag onto the floor. "I know it's not fair. New guys are supposed to get a week's orientation, not a patrol."

Bolan shrugged but didn't respond. He unlaced his boots, but didn't remove them. It was a trick he'd learned a long time ago.

"First thing, we'll get you a weapon and let you zero it before we move out. Chow will be served in about three hours. I'll come by and see if you're awake."

"Thanks." Bolan watched the man duck under the low beam that formed part of the door. There was a wall just outside the door made of sandbags and designed to absorb the shrapnel of a close hit. Bolan sat down on the cot and wondered how anyone could possibly sleep in there. Outside it was bad enough, but at least sometimes there was a breeze. The air was stagnant in the bunker, making Bolan think of a grave. Somehow that didn't seem to be the best environment in which to sleep.

He was surprised when Gibson woke him for the evening meal. He wasn't hungry, and he rolled over and went back to sleep. Before they came for him the next morning, he was awake, working on his rucksack, tossing out the things the Army thought he should carry and taking the stuff he knew he would need. Three canteens instead of one. No metal mess kit to rattle. Clean socks because the feet had to be kept dry, but no underwear because no one wore underwear in the jungle. He was using the little tricks he had learned throughout his career.

Gibson found Bolan sitting on the floor, working on the rucksack. "You about ready?"

"Breakfast?"

"Most assuredly. We'll stuff ourselves this morning, sucking down all the so-called orange juice and coffee we can drink. We need—"

"I'm familiar with the concept," Bolan said. LRRPs, Rangers and the Special Forces ate gigantic meals, stuffing themselves before long-range missions, living off the stored energy and moisture.

They left the bunker. "We're after one guy," Gibson told him. "Roams through the area killing anyone who crosses him. Doesn't matter. American or Vietnamese. Hell, I heard he killed a baby because the mother wouldn't cook his dinner. A real sweetheart."

The sun was just beginning to come up, the light reflecting off the water standing in the rice paddies below them. Smoke rose from the hootches, and there was movement in the fields as the farmers began their day.

"How are you going to know where to look for this guy?"

"Well, our intelligence isn't completely without resources, and it isn't always wrong. We've got a couple of reports that the guy's hanging out around the Trang My area. People there really hate him."

"He got a name?" Bolan asked.

"We don't have one for him. Just some local guy who's fairly good with a rifle, but he doesn't hang around to fight. Makes a shot, then gets the hell out. Terrorizes the villagers to get their cooperation."

"Great."

They ate a breakfast of scrambled eggs, toast, coffee and juice, eating as much as they could, stuffing it in and washing it all down. Then, feeling bloated, they drew an M-14 rifle for Bolan and took it to the makeshift range, where Bolan zeroed it. That done, he fired fifty rounds at targets spaced at a hundred, two hundred and four hundred meters. Satisfied, he cleaned it and drew two hundred rounds for the patrol.

"You want a pistol, too?"

"I've got one. Browning M-35 that I brought in from the States."

"Good choice."

"Seems like the best right now, but I could be convinced differently."

As they left the makeshift range, Gibson said, "Only thing wrong with those exotic weapons is finding the right ammunition for them."

"No problem in the Special Forces," Bolan stated. "I can get all the ammo I need there."

"Yeah, well . . ."

They found the rest of the patrol at the gate, a half-dozen men in faded fatigues, dirty boots and helmets. A couple of them wore flak jackets. Each had a couple of grenades, and one man packed a PRC-10 radio. Gibson inspected them, making sure they had everything needed for the patrol. He wondered why a soldier named Claiborne wanted to carry a dog-eared paperback. It was unnecessary weight, but if he wanted to tote it, then it was his business.

With that finished, they headed out, working their way through the wire until they reached the field of elephant grass that grew on the hillside, following a path that had been made by a dozen other, earlier patrols. That bothered Bolan because he had been told never to follow the same path twice, but nothing happened. Charlie hadn't sneaked close to set up booby traps. Once off the hill, they spread out, using the rice paddy dikes.

Bolan moved forward and touched Gibson on the shoulder. "Don't mean to tell you your business, but is this a good idea? I thought you walked through the paddies."

"Well, the farmers around here keep the dikes clear of booby traps, and if we stroll through the paddies, we crush the young plants and that alienates the farmers."

Bolan dropped back to his place in the patrol. They moved steadily, and he tried to figure out if it was hotter and more humid in Vietnam than in North Carolina. He'd have said that nothing could be worse than the late summer at Bragg, but now he wasn't sure. The sweat poured from him, soaking his fatigues. His mouth was filled with cotton, and although he'd only had three weeks' leave before coming to Vietnam, he felt out of shape. His breathing was in short, ragged gasps. He wished he hadn't eaten such a big breakfast and he wished he could sit down in the shade to rest. Except there wasn't any shade.

They came to a clump of palm, coconut and banana trees. The men spread out, forming a loose circle, and then sat down. Bolan collapsed in the center of the ring.

"It's the time shift," Gibson said sympathetically. "It takes a good two weeks to get adjusted to being twelve hours out of sync. In the World it's about midnight. That's why you're worn out, even though you slept through the night."

Bolan took a canteen and drank from it slowly. "Great."

"If you find yourself in real trouble, say something. We all went through this. The colonel shouldn't have sent you out so quickly."

There wasn't a thing Bolan could say to that. He put his canteen away and concentrated on resting. He ignored the sounds around him—jets and helicopters overhead and the distant boom of artillery and bombs. It was almost like being in the forests around Bragg, except that there were more aircraft in the sky.

They got through the rest of the day, circling to the south of Trang My. As they neared the village, they could see people working in the fields, while more people circulated among the hootches. A barking dog ran wild, smoke rose from the cooking fires, and a child cried noisily.

Gibson found a slight rise on the south side about fifty meters from the closest hootch. There was no other cover available, and when the men got onto their bellies, they were invisible in the short elephant grass. Bolan used a rotting log to brace his rifle.

They settled down to wait. No one moved, no one spoke. They ignored the calls of nature and the sudden thirst that came because they knew they couldn't drink. To move would be to show the enemy they were there, hiding. They lay in the baking heat of the tropical afternoon, sweating and burning, and letting only their eyes move as they searched for the sniper who was supposed to be coming at dusk. Insects attacked them, flies bit them, sipping their blood, but none of the men moved. They took it all, ignoring the discomfort, telling themselves that it was the enemy sniper who was causing their misery. If he hadn't been in the area killing Americans, they would be at their

camp drinking lukewarm beer and telling one another
about all the women they knew.

The situation remained static. The farmers remained in the fields; the women chased the kids; a
water buffalo bellowed; and someone hooted with
laughter. And yet something had changed. Subtly.
Bolan wasn't sure what it was. A feeling in the air, an
attitude of the people. Something.

He knew the sniper had slipped into the village unseen, come from another direction, using the cover.
Bolan kept his eyes moving, searching for a sign of the
sniper. Anything.

Then, among the hootches, Bolan saw a flash of
movement. A flash of green. And as he stared in that
direction, it came again. A quick movement, like a
man working his way through an enemy-held town.

The man stopped in front of a hootch, staring down
at the woman sitting there, working with a stone pes-
tle and chewing on betel nut. He held his rifle in one
hand, an old bolt-action weapon with a mounted
scope. Bolan was sure it was the standard sniper
weapon of the NVA, a Mosin-Nagant.

Without a word, Bolan slipped his weapon to his
shoulder and clicked off the safety at the front of the
trigger guard. It wasn't a particularly long shot. It was
one he could easily make, but he didn't fire right away.
There was something about shooting the enemy without giving him a chance. To ambush him when he least
expected it.

But then he remembered that this man had killed a
baby to make its mother obey his orders. The man had
demonstrated a lack of respect for human life and hu-

man values. Bolan hesitated no longer. He squeezed the trigger.

The shot ripped through the peaceful scene. People began to run, and the men of the patrol searched for targets. Bolan watched his bullet slam into the skull of the Vietcong sniper, shattering his head. Blood splashed on the side of the hootch as the man dropped. One leg kicked spasmodically, and one hand clutched at his rifle.

"Who fired?" Gibson demanded.

"I dropped your sniper," Bolan hissed, his voice low.

Gibson crawled over. "You sure?"

"Man with a rifle, down in the village. Bolt-action with a scope."

Gibson stared into the now-deserted village. He could see the single body, the blood spreading from the massive head wound. The rifle lay near by.

"Good shot."

"Thanks."

"Now we hang loose and see if his security team is with him. We'll take them, too, if we can."

As Gibson moved away, Bolan studied the dead man's body and wondered why it didn't bother him. He had just made his first kill in Vietnam and thought, perhaps, that he should regret the death of another human being.

But this was war. The man who had died deserved it. He was the enemy. He had killed American soldiers and would have done it again. Before he had gone into the field, he had understood the rules of the game. He had used his power and his weapons to intimidate the people, and had killed civilians to bend others to his will. Then he had walked into a village, carrying his weapon, identifying himself as an enemy soldier.

No, Bolan felt no regrets at pulling the trigger. There was a slight sense of satisfaction, a feeling that he had played the game under less than ideal circumstances and won. He should have been sitting in the camp, letting his body grow acclimatized to the environment in Vietnam.

They waited until dark, but no other soldiers showed themselves. Gibson thought that the security team, if it had been in the area, was now hoping to ambush the men who had killed their sniper. Gibson divided his squad into two teams, one for cover and one to check the body. Using the elephant grass and the hootches for cover, Bolan, Gibson and four others worked their way to the village.

While Bolan and the men spread out for security, Gibson searched the body. He found no papers or insignia hidden on the black pajamas. In the end, he could only take the weapon and the extra ammo the man had carried.

As they withdrew from the village, Gibson handed the sniper rifle to Bolan. "This is yours. You got him and you get his weapon."

Bolan grinned as he accepted the Mosin-Nagant. He didn't realize what it meant to his military career at that moment. He didn't know that it meant he wouldn't be joining a Special Forces A-Detachment as he had planned, but that he would be staying on at that hilltop camp. Soon Bolan would become a sniper specialist.

AND THEN HE WAS BACK in Bangkok, with the cab stopped in front of a run-down hotel tucked into a back street. The street was narrow and the crowds were thick, swirling along the sidewalks as people in open shops shouted out their wares.

"Good hotel," the driver said.

"You wait here."

"I wait."

Bolan stepped inside and walked to the desk. The man working there pretended not to understand English, but finally comprehended Bolan as money appeared. Having secured lodging, he went back out and paid off the driver. Then he went upstairs, avoiding the old elevator off the lobby.

The accommodations weren't the most modern in the world. There was no air-conditioning, but a ceiling fan rotated lazily overhead. The large bed had a mosquito net draped over it. The bathroom had a tub that stood on claw feet and had a rust stain near the drain. The lights in the room were dim, and flickered. Still, though, the room was more comfortable than a lot of places he had stayed.

Dropping his bag onto the bed, he sat down and wiped the sweat from his face. The first order of business would be to find a way into the black market so that he could buy the weapons he would need. He could, he knew, use the embassy to secure his weapons, but he didn't want any more people knowing his business. The fewer people involved, the better off he would be.

Bolan stood and moved to the window, which overlooked a narrow alley filled with garbage. Kids were swarming all over it, and a couple of adults were picking through it carefully.

No, thought Bolan, it didn't feel good to be back in Southeast Asia. Not good at all.

11

Rachel Jamison was waiting for McDonald when he arrived at her front door. Without a backward glance, or a shout to her mother, she hurried down the walk and waited for McDonald to open the passenger door.

Once in the car, she leaned close and said, "Hi, David Lee. I missed you."

McDonald dropped the car into gear. "I thought we could eat lunch at my place. A quick little lunch."

She grinned at him and nodded. "That would be nice." She slipped across the seat so that she was sitting next to him. When he put a hand on her knee, she sighed, sounding as though she'd never been happier.

McDonald sped up, dodging in and out of the noontime traffic, blowing the horn at the slow-moving bicycles and Hondas, cursing under his breath. He stopped once, got back into the flow of traffic, then turned toward his house.

Jamison kept him off balance. She guided his hand higher, letting his fingers brush at the skin of her bare thigh under her short skirt. When he touched her silk panties, she shivered.

He nearly drove off the road, and he had to force himself to concentrate on his driving. It was almost as if he'd forgotten how to drive and had to remind himself of every move.

But suddenly he was home, pulling into the driveway. He jammed on the brakes and leaped from the car, rushing around to open her door. He helped her out and nearly dragged her to the front door. The lock seemed to have shrunk. The key wouldn't fit. Finally he threw the door open and stepped inside. As he slammed it, he turned and pulled her into his arms, kissing her passionately. He felt her press herself against him, rubbing him with her hips.

"Now lunch?" he said breathlessly, hoping she wouldn't want to eat right at the moment.

She wedged a hand between their bodies, letting it dip lower, touching him. He sighed deeply, and she said, "Let's eat first."

"We can eat anytime," he muttered, as if he had just sprinted two hundred meters.

"But this will let the moment build. Anticipation can be very sweet."

He stepped back and looked at her. She was a beautiful, slender woman with long black hair, dark eyes and smooth, perfect skin. He reached out, touched her light blouse and slipped a hand inside.

"Later," she promised. "Later."

McDonald left her there, leaning against the front door. He dropped into the nearest chair and waited. Shutting his eyes, he grinned. "Okay. Later."

Together they moved into the small kitchen. McDonald started to prepare a lunch—cold cuts and raw vegetables taken from his refrigerator; two kinds of bread and beer, wine. He set the table, then held her chair for her.

He made himself a sandwich and sat down. "I'm not real hungry right now."

"Eat. It'll build up your strength for later. You won't collapse."

"Okay." McDonald picked up the sandwich and took a bite. "This isn't going to be easy."

"Then we'll have to do something to keep your mind off the afternoon. How was your day so far?"

"It's improving rapidly," McDonald said.

"But you must have done something this morning. You can't spend all your time thinking about me."

He felt her toes on his calf as she rubbed his leg under the table. He wanted to throw down his food and drag her into the bedroom, but he steadied himself.

"Well, interestingly enough, I was right. Remember last night I mentioned that I thought someone would be coming in, someone to search for the missing man?"

"Of course I remember."

"He's arriving today, or rather arrived."

She put down her sandwich. "Have you met him?"

"No. We're supposed to stay away from him. If he wants help, he'll have to come to us and ask for it."

"What is he going to do first?"

McDonald shrugged. "I don't know. It's his show. We might not even know when he leaves Bangkok. All I know is that he's here or will be. And that's all I did this morning. Learn about that."

Jamison stood and walked around the table until she was directly behind McDonald. She leaned over, her lips only inches from his ear, her hands on his chest.

"I don't think eating was such a great idea. Let's forget about lunch."

McDonald dropped his sandwich and stood. He grabbed her hand, taking her toward the bedroom. Once they were there, she pulled free and began to take off her clothes. She didn't want him to help but to sit there and watch as she peeled the garments seductively from her body. In seconds she was in front of him, naked and smiling. Staring at her glistening body, he forgot everything he had told her. Forgot that he was giving her secret information she had no business knowing. Forgot every aspect of his training in his hunger to have her. Which was just what she wanted.

BOLAN RESTED for a few minutes, then decided he'd better get out and see if he could hook into the black market. During his tours in Vietnam, it was easy to find black market goods. A few discreet questions in a couple of bars and someone would be able to direct him to the right place.

He dressed casually, but not too touristy, in blue jeans and a light short-sleeved shirt. He wore boots and felt naked without a weapon, but that was something that couldn't be helped. He'd have to trust that he could handle anything thrown at him until he could locate a supply of firearms.

He left the hotel and walked along the narrow streets past open shops that sold a variety of things. There was one merchant who specialized in fine blades, but Bolan wasn't interested in knives yet. After he secured the guns, he might be interested if the gun supplier didn't stock knives.

A section of the city that glowed with neon beckoned to him. Music vibrated from the buildings, shaking the windows and overpowering the roar of engines. The fumes seemed to hang over the city the way they did in L.A., Denver and Houston, giving the sunlight a golden glow but killing the trees and aiding in the destruction of the buildings.

Bolan found a honky-tonk that looked as if it had been lifted from a street in the United States. A Coors Beer sign burned in the window, surrounded by Miller Lite posters, and the music was rock and roll. Bolan opened the door and stepped into the dimness of the interior. After the brief sunlight, he had to squint in order to see.

When his eyes adjusted, he saw that he was in an ordinary tavern. A bar dominated one wall, and liquor bottles were stacked behind it. One corner held a small stage, where a slender girl who looked no older than fourteen swayed in time to music only she heard. Slowly she stripped until she was standing there naked, the sweat covering her body in a light, even coat. She paid no attention to anyone in the bar.

There was a group of small tables between the stage and the door, and a few men, most of them Oriental, sat drinking beer and smoking something that wasn't tobacco. Bolan moved to the bar, leaned on it and ordered a beer. He kept his eyes on the dancing girl as if nothing else in the place interested him.

The Executioner took his beer to one of the empty tables and sat down. Within seconds he was joined by a scantily clad woman. She leaned toward him, her elbows pressed together to deepen her cleavage. "Hey, you buy me drink?"

Bolan stared, as if evaluating her, then nodded. "Sure. Get whatever you want."

She waved at the bartender, who brought her a drink and waited there until Bolan paid for it. Four dollars. American. For colored water. But Bolan didn't care.

He turned his attention to the girl on the stage as she increased the tempo of her dance but still ignored the music blaring from the speakers fastened to the wall.

"You like. She come talk to you."

"No, you'll do fine."

Scooting her chair closer, she let her hand fall to his thigh, then began a slow massage of his leg as she rested her head against his shoulder. "You looking for good time?"

"I'm looking for a place to buy something—something you wouldn't have here."

"We have everything you want. You can have me. Or booze. Or maybe you want something to smoke."

"No. I need weapons."

She sat up as if she'd been poked in the side by something sharp. "Maybe you better leave."

"I have money. Lots of money."

Her eyes brightened. "You have money here? With you?"

"Do I look like I was born yesterday? No, I don't have it with me."

"You go."

"I'm willing to pay top dollar for a rifle and a pistol. No questions."

"You go."

Bolan finished his beer and stood. The woman kept her eyes on him as if he were a snake about to strike.

At the door he glanced back and saw that she was still watching him.

He had to go through the ritual three more times before he found someone who thought he could help. The girl at the table took Bolan into a back room, and they were joined by the bartender. He was a large man with thick black hair and had a round face with eyebrows that met over his nose. His thick shoulders and barrel chest were expected in an Oriental.

He came into the room, wiping his hands on a towel, which he tossed aside. Dropping into the chair opposite Bolan, he stared him in the eyes and said bluntly, "You looking for guns."

"I'd like a bolt-action rifle, a Remington Model 700. Pistol? An Israeli Desert Eagle, a Beretta 93-R, maybe a Browning M-35."

The man nodded slightly, but didn't speak. He jerked his head to the right, and the woman scampered from the room. The man then bent over and placed a bottle of whiskey on the table between them. "We drink."

Bolan wanted to refuse but knew he couldn't. To refuse would be to insult the man, and that would mean either a challenge to fight or a refusal of help.

The bartender opened the bottle, took a long pull and handed it to Bolan, who tilted it and drank deeply.

"How I know you not from the police?"

"Because the local police wouldn't be employing an American. Do you have what I need?"

"No," said the man. "I might know someone who can supply it, but it will take me a few hours. You come back at midnight."

Bolan stood and pulled a hundred-dollar bill from his pocket. He dropped it onto the table. "See you then."

Outside the bar, Bolan hesitated. The next problem was transportation. Ideally he would drive to the Cambodian border, cross in the middle of the jungle and walk to South Vietnam. The problem was the distance. It would take a month or more. Probably longer because he would have to move at night, which slowed the progress.

He started back to the hotel. If he could find someone to drive him across Cambodia, they could reduce travel time to a day at the most. In the States it would be a long afternoon, but then he wasn't in the States.

Bolan returned to his room to work out the problem. It was so damned maddening. Highway One started in Vietnam, in Saigon, crossed into Cambodia in the area American soldiers had called the Parrot's Beak, and continued all the way through Cambodia and into Thailand. One day's driving time and he would be there.

He thought about buying a motorcycle and running the highway after midnight, getting off about three or four in the morning. It might take a couple of days, but it was better than walking. And if he was spotted by guerrillas, he could probably get away cross-country.

Weapons and then a ride. That was the immediate problem. He just didn't know enough about smuggling people out of Cambodia and Vietnam. He'd heard the horror stories of yearlong treks through the jungle and chases by bandits and government soldiers until the refugees reached Thailand. There had been firefights between the Thais and the Cambodians as people tried to escape.

He folded his map and lay back on his bed, staring at the ceiling. It was possible that the man who was supplying the weapons would be able to help him get into Vietnam. Or take whatever help the embassy could provide. Neither solution appealed to him, though he felt better about trying to bribe someone than announcing his intentions at the embassy. Too many leaks there.

He decided to take a short nap, and he awakened later in a darkened room—hot, hungry and thirsty. He lifted his watch and stared at the glowing numbers. There was about an hour until his rendezvous at the bar.

Bolan got up, stripped and took a shower. Feeling refreshed, he dressed and headed out. Rather than go straight to the bar, he wandered the streets, watching the people around him, looking for a tail. Although he saw a couple of the same people on several occasions, no one seemed overly interested in him.

He stopped at the door of the bar, took a deep calming breath and walked in, hoping that he wasn't walking into a trap.

DIEM SAT BEHIND HIS DESK, the lantern throwing out a white glow while he waited for one of the men to fix the generator. He had his feet propped on his desk as he read through a number of documents sent to him from Hanoi. They were propaganda, telling him of the great leaps made by the government in improving the life of the citizens of the Socialist Republic of Vietnam. Diem looked at the rough furniture and at the lantern he had stolen from the Americans years before, and wondered how accurate the document could be.

There was a knock at the door and one of his guards looked in. "Comrade, there is a messenger here from Ho Chi Minh City."

Diem dropped his feet to the floor and sat up. He set the papers aside. "Send him in."

The man entered and stopped in front of the desk. "A secret communication. You must sign for it."

Diem took the envelope and checked the number stamped in the corner. On the sheet handed him he found the same number and wrote his name, along with the date and time, then gave it back.

"Thank you, Comrade."

"If your duties don't demand an immediate return to the city, please use our facilities to refresh yourself."

The man nodded. "You are very kind." He whirled and left, escorted by the guard who had brought him.

Diem stared hard at the envelope, but then ripped it open and extracted the single sheet it contained.

The report was from the agents in Bangkok. Diem read it quickly, then grinned. Already the Americans were sending more people. Someone had arrived in Bangkok to learn the fate of the agent Thomas Ryan. The document stated that nothing else was known other than that the man had arrived.

Now Diem got up and hurried from his hootch. He found the messenger in the mess hall drinking tea with the guard. As he approached, both men stood. The colonel waved for them to sit down, saying, "I would like you to carry a message back with you when you go.''

"Yes, Comrade.''

"When you have finished your tea, please come by my office.''

Diem turned and fled the heat of the mess hall. The open fire in the stone-and-clay fireplace at the end of the building kept the temperature high, and meals taken there seldom held any pleasure. The colonel could feel the perspiration beading his forehead.

When he returned to his office and sat down behind the desk, he scribbled a message to the headquarters in the heart of Ho Chi Minh City, directing them to do everything to ensure that the American agent found his way from Thailand to Vietnam. Diem wanted the man to come to him. They didn't need to try to find him as he worked his way across Kampuchea and into Vietnam. They could sit back and let him come to them because they knew what his final destination would be. Diem suggested that all patrols be pulled back and told not to intercept him.

For a moment he wondered if he was being too clever. If the man had no trouble getting into Vietnam, he might suspect a trap. But then he decided that the man would suspect nothing. The American would congratulate himself on his cleverness at avoiding the enemy, and praise his good fortune. He would walk right into the jaws of death.

Having finished the message, Diem poured himself a glass of wine. He looked at the wall where the pictures hung, let his eyes roam over them, starting at the end where there was a tiny poor-quality black-and-white photo of himself as a young man setting out on the journey to the South. Then on to the pictures that marked his military career, the quality of the photos improving after he'd stolen the camera from the body of a South Vietnamese ranger.

Finally he came to the wanted poster of the Executioner, a line drawing of the man who had once roamed Vietnam killing high-ranking Vietcong and North Vietnamese officers, a man who had attacked from hiding, shooting men in the back.

Diem knew that his anger at the Executioner's method was artificial because he had done the same. Being a sniper meant attacking the enemy from hiding. But it also meant harming the enemy.

The colonel lifted his glass in salute to the Executioner and spoke out loud. "You were one of the best. Someday I'll kill you. I wish they were sending you."

He sipped his wine, knowing that the odds the Executioner was returning to Vietnam were remote. But he could hope for the best.

12

Bolan had been at the table long enough to chase away one bar girl who wanted to have a drink and promised to show him a good time. He had also been able to get one warm beer and to watch the three girls on the stage compete for the attention of the men in the audience. Each stripped quickly, not wasting time by trying to be subtle about it. The smoke hung heavy in the air, and the driving beat from the speakers rocked the room. The crowd was roaring at the dancers and at one another. Bolan was reminded of a hand-to-hand fight.

The skinny, short man sat down at the table without waiting for an invitation from Bolan. He snapped his fingers at a waitress, the sound lost in the vibrating din. When she finally looked at him, he waved her over and yelled his order into her ear. As she retreated, the man studied Bolan.

His sweaty face was pockmarked from a bad case of acne. Or maybe the scars had been the result of a mild case of smallpox when he was a child. The black hair was slicked down heavily and combed straight back. The collar of the shirt was frayed and there was dirt under the man's fingernails. Obviously he was an intermediary sent to size up Bolan before the final transaction was made.

When his drink arrived, he peeled off a bill from a huge roll of fairly low denominations. As the waitress retreated, he grabbed at her skirt, flipping it up so that he could see her panties. He picked up his drink, held it high as if examining its contents, then nodded at Bolan. He took a long drink, then leaned forward to shout across the table as he burped loudly.

"You look for special merchandise?"

The accent was so heavy that Bolan could barely understand him. The blasting rock music didn't help communication. Before answering, Bolan glanced at the bartender, the man who had met with Bolan in the back room earlier in the day.

The bartender was standing as close to them as the bar would allow. When he saw Bolan's glance, he nodded once and returned to his duties.

"Yeah."

"Why you want these fancy things? Maybe you not like men who grow poppy. Maybe you DEA."

Bolan shook his head. "No."

"Maybe you get these things and go after my friend in the mountain."

Bolan shrugged. "If I was with the DEA, don't you think I'd have another source for the merchandise? I wouldn't have to buy it on the streets."

"Maybe this your cover."

"Maybe you're just blowing smoke."

The man sat back, looking as if he'd been hit. He blinked rapidly, then shouted, "I not understand this blowing smoke."

"It means I don't think you can help me. It means you're wasting my time."

The man snorted and nodded. "You think that? You just wait to see." He was silent for a moment, then added, "What you want with these things? Where you go?"

"Do you have to ask?"

"I must protect friend."

The last thing Bolan wanted to do was share the information with a man he didn't know and didn't trust. But there was no reason for Bolan to tell the truth, either. "Let's just say I'm going on a trip, and I want to protect myself from the wild animals that inhabit the jungle."

"Ho-ho. That very good. You worry about tiger?"

"Jackals."

"I think maybe we not be able to do business. I don't like you."

Now Bolan grinned. "And I don't like you, but you tell me what kind of a dent I could put in anyone's operation with the limited resources I've asked for."

The man seemed to consider that. He finished his drink, spilling some of it down his chin, then slapped the table and shouted, "You right. We go."

"Where?"

"To warehouse to make business. You bring money?"

"I have some, yes. More at my hotel if I need it." Bolan stood and dropped some money onto the table. He waited for the man to pass him, then followed him into the humid night.

There were few lights along the crowded street, and Bolan was worried about an ambush, especially when they left the crowds behind. The man and his cronies might have decided for a straight rip-off unless Bolan convinced them that more money would be available later if they cooperated. They didn't have to know that this was a one-of-a-kind mission and that he didn't plan to return to Bangkok.

The Thai turned into an alley, and Bolan paused at the entrance. Piles of garbage littered the ground. A couple of cans had been filled to overflowing, so the people who lived in the surrounding buildings merely threw their trash onto the ground. One side of the alley had a blank wall, but the other had four or five doors. A single light bulb above one created a pool of light about halfway to the end of the alley—almost the perfect place for an ambush if it hadn't been for the light.

"You come, or you afraid?"

Bolan could see nothing out of place. There were no suspicious shadows, no real hiding places for the ambushers and no indication that an ambush had been laid. At least there was none in the alley. He followed the man who had walked to the illuminated entryway.

"Okay, Joe, we go inside. Down stair. I go first, but you stay close. People upstair not like visitor, and they trigger-happy."

"Lead on," Bolan said.

His contact opened the door onto a dimly lit landing and two flights of stairs, one going up and one going down. Those leading down looked as if they'd been carved out of rock. The walls bowed outward slightly and dripped with moisture—the perfect environment to ensure that any weapons stored below would rust quickly.

At the bottom of the steps there was a series of tunnels that led off in four directions. The Thai moved to the mouth of one and flicked a switch. Lights came on the length of the tunnel, revealing a wide area, maybe twelve or fourteen feet across that was lined with crates holding weapons and ammunition. They were stacked to the ceiling, twelve or fourteen feet above the floor. One niche bore racks of weapons—everything from M-16s and AK-47s to newer assault rifles, including the AK-74. There were also grenade launchers and M-60 machine guns locked in with Soviet-made RPDs. And at the far end, standing by itself, was a 20 mm antiaircraft gun known as a ZSU-33.

"You planning to start a war?" Bolan asked.

"I am businessman. Provide service for those who not have guns. Now, what you have in mind?"

"I was hoping for a Remington 700 with a Redfield variable power scope. It was used by the Marine Corps during the war."

"I know weapon. Have many. Come."

They moved deeper into the tunnel. The crates were stamped with U.S. Army markings and Soviet military insignia. There were crates from France, China and Vietnam, ammo manufactured in Israel and Germany. It was an international clearing house for weapons.

"You have any antitank guns?"

The man stopped and looked back. "Such as?"

"Nothing. I was just wondering."

"I able to supply variety. You tell me what you want, I find it."

As they moved deeper into the warehouse, Bolan noticed that the air was cool but no longer damp. He could hear the hum of air-conditioning, which might have held the dehumidifier. That would inhibit the rusting of the weapons and provide a safe environment for the huge stockpiles of ammunition. Whoever ran the warehouse knew what he was doing.

They stopped at a rack that held several bolt-action rifles, including the old M1903A4, the Mosin-Nagant and a Mauser Model SP66. There were several different types of sniper rifles from several different manufacturers. Bolan crouched in front of the rack and studied the weapons. All were clean and lightly oiled, and there was no evidence of rust or dirt. Someone was taking good care of his merchandise.

"You ask for Remington?"

"Yeah."

The man removed a key ring from his pocket and unlocked the rack. Then he stepped back to let his customer examine the weapons. Bolan picked up one of the Remingtons, worked the bolt, then looked down the barrel. Like the rest of the weapon, it was clean. There was no evidence of pitting. The bolt worked smoothly, and the trigger pull was even. It was a beautiful weapon.

"How much?"

"You said you wanted pistol?"

"Yes. The Israeli Desert Eagle in .44 Magnum, if you have it. If not, a Browning."

The arms dealer moved down to a group of crates and popped one open. Inside were a dozen Desert Eagles. The man extracted one and handed it to Bolan.

Again the Executioner examined the weapon, working the slide, checking the safeties and the trigger pull. No sign of rust. The weapon had been well cared for. The Desert Eagle was a heavy weapon whose extra weight was designed to dampen the recoil. It wasn't the sort of pistol to hump through the jungle with for days, but it was a good handgun to have if you didn't have to backpack it, the ammo and all kinds of other supplies. He dropped the magazine into his hand, then slapped it home again.

"It chambered for .357," said the Thai. "Hold nine in magazine and one in chamber."

"You have any of the .44 Magnums?"

The man grinned and bowed slightly. "I afraid we not able to purchase any larger gun."

"How much for the Remington, this pistol and two hundred rounds for each?"

"Five thousand dollar."

Bolan laughed shortly. "I need the weapons, but not so badly that I'll let you rob me. Two thousand."

"Price not negotiable. Five thousand dollar."

"All prices are negotiable. I don't mind you making a profit, but you're being ridiculous. Two thousand."

The man rubbed his chin, then laughed. "You right. All price negotiable. Everything you want, plus a good knife, Kabar or Gerber, and four hand grenade for five thousand."

Bolan sat on one of the crates, the pistol in his hand. "Your offer is tempting. Especially the knife. I'd like it, without the grenades for twenty-five hundred."

"Forty-five hundred. No grenade."

"Three thousand," Bolan countered.

"Four thousand?"

"Split the difference for thirty-five hundred, cash, and you've got a deal."

"Maybe thirty-seven fifty?" the man suggested.

Bolan stood and held out a hand. "Thirty-seven fifty if you provide a case for the rifle and a holster for the handgun. A shoulder rig. And a survival pack. Freeze-dried food for a week. Whatever you have."

"Done!" The Thai moved to another case, taking out boxes holding fifty rounds apiece. He pushed four of them to the side and then gave Bolan two extra magazines for the Desert Eagle.

Bolan didn't wait. He loaded one of the magazines, slapped it into the butt and jacked a round into the chamber. He slipped the pistol into his belt, feeling better now that he was armed.

They returned to the rack of rifles, and Bolan selected the Remington that he wanted. As the man searched for the ammo, the Executioner asked, "You have a range so that I can zero it?"

"You rent range for one hour, two hundred dollar and we keep brass."

"Everything has a price."

The man faced Bolan. "I am businessman. Why I give anything away when I able to sell it?"

"Good point."

The man picked up a couple of boxes of ammo and said, "You follow me."

They entered another of the tunnels and traveled about one hundred meters before reaching a waist-high counter. When the man touched a light switch, the range appeared at a perpendicular angle. Bolan set his rifle on the counter, then drew the pistol, setting it next to the Remington. There were ear protectors hanging on the partition that separated the firing stations from one another.

"You need guide?" the Thai asked.

"Guide?"

"For trip. You need help finding way into jungle?"

"I might be in need of some help crossing a border or two, if that's what you have in mind."

"Maybe I able to help you. You work on weapon, I make phone call. For one thousand dollar I can find you guide."

"You do that."

As the man disappeared, Bolan picked up the Desert Eagle, and checked it over. He hauled in a target, then wheeled it out to the twenty-five meter range, using the rope and pulley near his head. That done, he slipped off the safety and aimed. He moved his hands slightly, searching for the position that was the most comfortable. When he was ready, he squeezed the trigger gently.

The pistol crashed, but the sound was dampened by the ear protectors. The recoil wasn't as great as he had expected, the weight of the weapon absorbing some of it. The brass kicked out to the right, hit the wall and bounced away.

Bolan squeezed off another five rounds and pulled the target closer so that he could check the results. The weapon was pulling to the right and high. He adjusted the sights and tried again. This time the rounds were clustered in a tight group in the center of the black.

He reloaded and set the target at fifty meters, which was extreme range for a pistol, but he wanted an idea of how tight the group would hold at the extended range.

When he looked at the target, he was pleased. The Desert Eagle didn't scatter the shots as some other pistols did. He could count on it for long-range shooting, if it ever became necessary.

That finished, he reloaded and set the pistol down. He brought in a target, checked it and ran it out to two hundred meters, which was the limit of the range. He would have preferred sighting it in at five hundred meters, but that didn't seem to be possible.

He picked up the Remington. The weight and feel was familiar. After his first couple of missions using the M1903A4, the Army had managed to get a couple of the Remingtons that had been modified for the Marine Corps. Bolan never knew whether it was an official trade, or if someone had swapped for them outside of channels. Not that it mattered, because the weapon was there and it was superior to the old sniper rifles.

He worked the bolt again and loaded it. Bolan was so familiar with the weapon that he could have done it with his eyes closed. He'd carried it in combat for six months, lived with it and learned to fieldstrip it blindfolded. His fingers hadn't forgotten those long-ago lessons.

The Executioner wrapped the sling around his arm, leaned forward, resting an elbow on the counter. The Remington fit his shoulder well, the stock resting against his cheek. He sighted through the scope, keeping his head back so that the recoil wouldn't slam the rim of the scope into his face. It felt good to hold the weapon again.

He sighted on the target and squeezed the trigger. In that moment Bolan wasn't on an underground range in Bangkok—he was back in Vietnam. It was no longer cool, but hot and humid. The air smelled of rain, dust and death. The "range" was five hundred meters long, and Bolan was lying in the hot sun, the new Remington in his hands.

He fired again, the sound echoing through the cavernous rifle range. Through the scope, Bolan could see the bullet hole dead center in the black.

And then, with his third shot, his mind was in Vietnam as he stood up and began the slow walk to retrieve the target.

13

The five shots clustered in the center could have been covered by a quarter. The weapon fired true.

As Bolan left the range, Sergeant Gibson intercepted him. He stopped, blinking in the bright sunlight. "You ready to go out for a couple of days?"

Bolan shook his head. "I've been in barely twenty-four hours. Thought I got a few more." He wiped the sweat from his face with the sleeve of his uniform, leaving a ragged, wet stain.

"I know, but we've gotten word that the Rifleman is back at it. We think we've located his AO so that we can flood the area with our people and maybe pick him off."

"How many are going out?"

"Ten teams. Two snipers per team, or rather a sniper and a spotter, plus security."

"Okay," Bolan said. "How soon?"

"We'd like to get everyone into the field in two hours."

"It'll take me that long to get my weapon cleaned and get my gear together."

Gibson put a hand to his eyes to shade them. Sweat dripped from his chin and the end of his nose. "Then you can go with the last team. You got a preference for spotter?''

Bolan slung the rifle and held on to the strap. He was quiet for a moment. "Corporal Whitney."

"I wanted him to go out with Tilman. Figured he'd keep Whitney out of trouble."

"Whatever."

"Okay, you can have him, but don't say I never did anything for you."

Bolan began moving up the hill toward his hootch. Gibson tagged along, but didn't say anything until they reached the entrance to the bunker.

"See me before you go out if you get the chance. I'll brief Whitney on your AO."

"Sure." Bolan ducked and stepped into the bunker that was his hootch. It was dim inside, and he stood there for a moment letting his eyes adjust to the darkness. When he could see again, he moved to his bunk and sat down. He set the rifle on the floor, then rocked back, stretching out. As he unbuttoned his fatigue jacket, he blew on his chest to cool himself.

It was a miserable country, hot and full of flies and mosquitoes. The people wanted nothing to do with either side fighting the war. The government in Saigon wanted the United States to win the war for them, but then put roadblocks in the way. The news media didn't care for anything or anyone other than their story, and they weren't above making one up if nothing surfaced.

Given all that, Gibson still expected him to go into the field and risk death. Go into the field where he would have to lie still for days, eating C-rations that wouldn't be served to convicts. The ACLU would file suit to prevent such cruel and inhuman punishment. He would have to lie there, not moving, hoping the enemy would walk by, and once he had returned, no one would thank him. They would look at him through hooded eyes, believing that he was crazy.

And the sad thing was that Bolan wasn't sure they weren't right. Why would a man go through this? Why not go to Crawford and demand a transfer into a Special Forces A-Detachment. Why not call the Fifth Special Forces in Nha Trang and let them know he had been spirited away to this rotting mountain to become a sniper. Fifth would probably have him off the hill by nightfall.

Instead, he sat up, took the cleaning kit from the nightstand made from an old ammo crate and began to clean his weapon. He worked on it carefully, lovingly, because it was the one thing he could count on to save his life. Men might fail him, the system might fail him, but the rifle would not. If he took care of it, it would take care of him. In Remington he trusted and that was all.

He finished the job but didn't load the rifle. He would do that just before he left the hootch. He turned and picked up his rucksack, checking to make sure no one had stolen anything from it. Real soldiers wouldn't steal from one another, but the men who never went into the field sometimes took souvenirs, not realizing that men's lives depended on the equipment they had with them.

As he was finishing up, there was a tap on the beams that held in place the sandbags forming the entrance to the bunker. A voice called out, "Bolan? You in there?"

"I'm here."

Corporal Whitney entered. He was a short man who was going prematurely bald. Or maybe the stress of Vietnam was stealing his hair. He had a gaunt look, as if he hadn't eaten in a month. His cheekbones were sharp, as was his chin. Although he was well trained and could hump the boonies all day, he looked as if a strong wind would blow him over.

He crouched in front of Bolan, the sweat stains on his fatigues circled by large salt rings. He had his gear with him, complete to the knife taped to the shoulder harness and the pistol belt with two canteens hooked onto it. He'd brought the binoculars and his XM-21 sniper rifle. "You about ready, Sarge?"

Bolan shook his head. "Is anyone ready for this? Ready as I'll ever be." He stood and began to shoulder his rucksack, Whitney helping him get it seated on his shoulders. Bolan buckled the pistol belt and picked up his rifle. "Let's get going."

Bolan and Whitney moved into the bright sunlight, descending the hill to the gate where the security squad waited. Bolan recognized a couple of the men. "Haven't scared you off yet, huh?"

"Hell, Sarge," one answered. "Your missions are the only ones where we make contact. At least we hurt Charlie when we go out on these."

"Glad to have you." He looked at the two men he didn't know. "Anyone have any questions?"

When none were asked, he said, "Remember, this isn't a regular patrol. We maintain absolute noise discipline at all times. No talking, no smoking and no grabass. We hit the weeds and we're still chilly. No one moves. No one talks. No one scratches his butt. Your job is to protect my ass. I'll zap the dinks. If you have problems with that, pull out now and I'll get a replacement for you."

No one spoke. "Let's move out." He cocked a thumb at Whitney. "You take the point. Guterriera, you have trail. Let's go."

They walked through the gate, through the gaps in the wire and across the open fields of elephant grass. When they reached the jungle, they slowed but kept moving, slipping through the trees and among the bushes. They tried not to leave signs, although there had been so many patrols through this part of the jungle that it didn't matter that much.

They kept at it, working their way deeper, the pace slowing as the jungle became more dense. And then it opened up again until it looked like a well-manicured park. There was very little undergrowth—just short grass that covered the ground like a thick green carpet. The broad branches of the hardwood trees locked together high above them to form a canopy that held out the sun and the rain but held in the humidity, creating a steam bath. It was like trying to walk through a hothouse wrapped in a wet towel.

They stopped once for rest, moving out quickly again. They arrived at the edge of the jungle and crossed an open field that was crisscrossed with rice paddies, some of them filled with water, which gave the clearing a checkerboard appearance. They used the dikes, moving along them carefully. But the whole system was well traveled so that the enemy couldn't spread booby traps without killing more farmers than American soldiers. Besides, the farmers removed them as quickly as the VC planted them.

They crossed into the tree line again, reaching another open area around dusk. Spread out before the squad were a couple of hills, some farmers' hootches and one tiny hamlet hidden in a dense copse that protected it from the sun and rain. People were going about their daily business, some in the rice paddies, some working around their hootches, cooking the evening meal.

Bolan spread his men out in a defensive circle, then crouched at the edge of the bush. He watched the people below him, but could see nothing out of the ordinary—which didn't mean the enemy wasn't close, only that there was no obvious evidence of them.

"Have the men eat in shifts now," Bolan whispered to Whitney. "Half eating, half on guard. We won't get a chance to rest again until morning."

Whitney nodded and crawled off to tell the security team. Bolan took out his canteen and sipped from it. He didn't want a lot of water, just enough to kill his thirst. He avoided the C-rations that he carried.

The sunset and the light vanished. Music from a Saigon radio station drifted across the valley on the evening breeze. The fires went out one by one, and lights from the hootches disappeared until there was no light from below, just various shades of gray and black. A water buffalo bellowed, and artillery rumbled in the distance.

The mosquitoes came out and attacked the men, but they ignored them. They didn't swat them, but rather let them drink their fill. Bolan refused to let the men use any of the standard-issue insect repellent because the enemy could smell it. They would find the Americans because of the odor from the repellent. They could literally smell out an ambush.

But soon it was after midnight, and no one was moving in the valley. It was quiet, with only the occasional rumble from night bombings and artillery. Bolan was up, moving into the valley, his men spread out behind him. They moved slowly, trying not to silhouette themselves against the sky.

Skirting the edge of the valley, they kept the jungle close to them in case they had to retreat to the cover. Bolan was leading them to one of the hills on the east side of the valley where there would be good cover. There he would be able to see everything that moved in the valley, and if the Rifleman appeared he would have a shot at him.

The security team was spread out on the other side of the hill, watching another, smaller valley to the east. There were fingers of jungle reaching into it, making it a good place for the enemy to hide. But Whitney was convinced the VC would operate in the larger area because there was more food to steal and more people available to exploit.

Bolan found a good blind and settled into it, telling Whitney to check on the security team to make sure they'd taken good, well-concealed positions. Whitney forced them to adjust the foliage in their cover so that it didn't stand out. He also told them to change it at first light, then not touch it until dusk.

At dawn the valley came alive again. The people began to move into the fields, but the enemy didn't show. Bolan lay quietly, his canteen near his hand, along with extra ammo for the rifle. If he spotted the Rifleman, he didn't want to get caught short.

Whitney was only a couple of meters away, the binoculars to his eyes. He scanned the valley slowly, methodically searching for a change that would mark the intrusion of the enemy. Each time he finished a scan, he rested his head on his arms and closed his eyes. After five minutes or so, he began another search.

Bolan used the scope to make spot checks and to figure the ranges to various targets on the valley floor. Knowing the distance to the objects might save him precious seconds when the target appeared.

The sun climbed into the sky, and while the heat had been uncomfortable during the night, it became almost unbearable now. The sun baked them, and sweat soaked their uniforms quickly. Dehydration was a very real possibility. Their source of water was limited, so it became a game of drinking just enough without wasting it.

Bolan tried to ignore the growing heat. He felt the sun burning through his fatigues, and his skin seemed to be on fire. Tiny flies buzzed around his face, diving at the beads of perspiration, but he didn't flick them away. The flash of movement would betray his position. Now it was patience that would beat the enemy.

Clouds boiled on the horizon, promising rain and relief from the sun. Bolan prayed for rain, although it would help the enemy. It would cut visibility to a fraction of what it was now. He wouldn't be able to see the far rim of the valley, but at that moment he didn't care.

And then he did. There was a flicker of movement across from them, a furtive movement as if someone were skirting the edge of the jungle. Bolan trained his scope on it.

"To the west, about one o'clock, at the edge of the trees," he hissed.

Slowly Whitney turned until his binoculars were focused on that one patch of jungle. He studied the area and whispered, "I think I've got him."

"VC or farmer."

"VC. He's got a weapon. Long rifle. Not short like the SKS. Could be our boy."

Bolan rocked to his left and wrapped the sling of the rifle around his arm. He worked the bolt, making sure the round was seated properly, then made sure the safety was off. Since he wasn't going to be moving now until after he fired, he didn't need it. Nothing irked a sniper more than to slowly pull at the trigger, increase the tension until the muscles popped and the veins stood out under the strain, then realize the safety was on.

Using his scope, he spotted his adversary for a brief moment. He'd seen the Rifleman only once, but he knew he would never forget the man's face. He tried to get a glimpse at the enemy with the rifle, but the VC eluded him, staying just inside the trees as he worked his way toward the valley floor.

Then the man appeared at the edge of the jungle, crouching on one knee, his rifle held in his right hand. Through the scope, Bolan could make out the face. The Rifleman looked tired and sweaty. He didn't seem to be the same relaxed soldier Bolan had seen before.

"Twelve hundred meters," Whitney said. "Wind blowing from left to right at eight to ten kilometers per hour. It'd be one hell of a shot, if you made it."

"We'll wait." At that range, the shot would take almost two seconds to get to the target. Any movement by the enemy would mean a miss. Not to mention the breeze that would mean he'd have to guess at the windage. At twelve hundred meters, that much wind could mean the bullet would move as much as a half meter off center.

The Rifleman turned and waved to the men behind him in the jungle. They joined him and began to work their way down the hillside, moving toward the hamlet that was only eight hundred meters away. They stuck to the cover available, using it well. Bolan lost sight of them periodically, only to have them reappear lower on the slope.

"That's it," he whispered just loud enough for Whitney to hear. "Come to Papa."

No one else seemed to have seen the Vietcong patrol as it swept down the hillside. The farmers worked their fields without glancing up, but then they'd had years of practicing their skills at not seeing anything they shouldn't. Those who saw too much tended to disappear in the night, or find themselves caught in the middle of firefights.

The VC reached the hamlet and spread out. A few women who had been inside, suddenly appeared and sat down together in the center of the hamlet. One of the enemy soldiers stood to the side, watching them.

The VC worked their way through the village, gathering supplies. Some of the men dragged burlap bags of rice to the center of the hamlet where the women waited, stacking them up. Through his rifle's scope, Bolan could see the "shaking hands" symbol that marked rice provided by the United States. The

American taxpayer was now supplying food for the Vietcong, as well as the villagers.

The enemy soldiers gathered there in a rough half circle. The Rifleman stood with one foot on a bag of rice, his weapon clutched in the crook of his elbow, the muzzle pointed down. He watched as one of the VC soldiers stormed around, waving his arms, apparently yelling at the peasants.

"I'm going to take him now," Bolan said. "Once I've fired, use your weapon and drop as many as you can. I'll be watching my man, making sure he's dead."

"Got it."

"You don't fire until I do."

There was no reply to that. Bolan centered the cross hairs on the chest of the Rifleman. He could see everything about the man—see that his clothes were soaked with sweat, see that he wore a round canteen draped over one shoulder.

A final time, he checked the windage, guessed at it and cranked it into the scope so that he could aim at the man's chest. The range was between eight and nine hundred meters. A long shot, but Bolan didn't think he'd get another crack.

"Shooting," he said to warn Whitney, then began the slow squeeze on the trigger. Just as the weapon fired, the man far below moved. The round hit him, but high, maybe in the shoulder or in the side or maybe just in the arm. The man dropped to the ground as if he had been killed. But then he rolled to the right behind the bags of rice.

Whitney opened fire, using his XM-21. The modified M-14 bucked as he shot on semiauto, throwing out rounds as quickly as he could find targets and pull the trigger. They were slamming into the walls of the hootches, kicking up clouds of dust. A couple of men fell, one of them spurting blood.

"Missed him," Bolan grunted. He rolled to the right, trying to get a better angle. Through the scope he saw a foot and fired at it, but the shot was wide. Dirt boiled into the air.

Then the man was up and running, holding his rifle in one hand. Bolan fired, trying to lead him. The round smashed into the side of a hootch, and as it did, the Rifleman dived through the door.

"Missed him," Bolan said again.

Rifle fire erupted in the hamlet. The men with the Rifleman were shooting with their AKs, but the range was too great. Bolan heard one crack by his head, but that was the only one that even came close.

He focused his attention on the hootch where the Rifleman hid. Bolan knew he couldn't expect the man to come out the front and into the sunlight. He could easily kick his way through a wall and disappear into the trees, but Bolan didn't think he would. The challenge had been made. One man against the other. Nothing else mattered.

The shot caught him off guard. The dirt in front of him exploded, throwing up a cloud of obscuring dust. Bolan shifted around, but the man was gone. Touching the back of his hand to his lips, he kept his eye pressed to the scope. He caught a flash of movement and fired, knowing he would hit nothing.

To his left, Whitney continued to fire slowly, keeping the heads of most of the enemy soldiers down. Bursts of firing came from the hamlet—the Rifleman's security team was trying to protect him—but the shots came nowhere near either of them.

Bolan spotted the Rifleman, holding his arm at a strange angle. Before he could shoot, the man vanished into a hootch. The American sniper reloaded, but when he looked down again, the man was on the move, running across a narrow open space. There was no chance of hitting him.

"He's hurt," Bolan said, "but I can't put him down." He tried to get off a shot, but the Rifleman wouldn't stop to give Bolan a chance to kill him.

"I think it's about time we got out of here," Whitney put in.

"No, not yet. We've got some time left. We have to be patient."

Bolan studied the scene. The Rifleman popped up, fired and disappeared again.

But then came another and another. Bolan ducked and rolled. He glanced through the scope and squeezed off a shot, knowing he had no hope of hitting the enemy.

Something suddenly slammed into the side of his rifle. It spun from his hands, the barrel bent and the stock exploding. Bolan felt the splinters catch him in the hands and face. He grunted in surprise.

Whitney was next to him immediately. "You okay?"

Bolan scrambled after his rifle. The scope was smashed. The barrel bent at an angle and part of the stock was gone. "That's it."

"We get out now?"

"We get out." He picked up the rifle, not wanting to leave the enemy anything they might be able to use. "Go."

Whitney began to crawl up the hillside, working his way to the summit. Once there, he used the radio to alert the security team that they were coming in.

As Bolan joined him, he said, "Security says they've picked up no movement."

"I hit him," Bolan said. "I hit him, but not hard enough."

"We could call in artillery. There's a good chance we could get him with artillery."

"But we'd never know. Besides, we'd kill most of the innocent people down there. We can get him on another day."

They called to the security team and stopped. Bolan sat up and pulled at a couple of splinters that stuck out of his left hand and shoulder. "Someone get on the point and head to the jungle. We'll halt there to see if there's any pursuit."

"You think we have to worry about that?" Whitney asked.

"No. They'll lick their wounds and fade from the countryside just as we're going to do. This one is a draw, but we'll get another chance at him."

But there had been no more chances at the Rifleman. It was the draw of the cards that kept Bolan from finally getting the enemy sniper.

BOLAN LOOKED at the Remington 700 he held in his hands. If he hadn't seen the first one destroyed in Vietnam, he would have thought that he held the same rifle. It was a good weapon.

He finished zeroing it, then unloaded it. He'd have to buy something from the Thai man and clean the rifle in his room. Do it right, because if he took care of his weapon, it would take care of him.

There was an echoing of footsteps as two people approached him. Bolan set the rifle on the counter and picked up the Desert Eagle, making sure it was loaded and that the safety was off before he set it down. He turned to face the entrance of the tunnel, but kept his hand close to the weapon.

Two figures appeared—the Thai and a woman. He said something to her, but his voice was lost in the echoes. She nodded as they came forward.

Bolan waited patiently, wondering what was going on now. The man had promised him a guide, not a female companion. She was a good-looking woman— tall and slim with long black hair. Her fine features almost made her look Occidental.

"I have brought you a guide for a thousand dollar finder's fee."

"No," Bolan said. "I travel fast."

"So do I," the woman replied. "Fast and smart."

Bolan stared at her, but she didn't drop her eyes. She stared back at him, waiting. "I can get you anywhere you want to go," she promised. She winked at him. "I have no trouble crossing any borders that we might need to cross."

"I'll bet you don't."

"One thousand dollars," the Thai repeated.

"I'll pay your fee, if you provide me with a cleaning kit for the weapons."

"Done."

"I'll talk to your guide, but I don't think I'll need her."

"You'll find that you do," the man said. "She has a knowledge of all of Southeast Asia and you can get where you want to go the fastest way possible."

Bolan picked up his pistol and tucked it into his waistband. He took his rifle and made sure it was unloaded. "You promised a carrying case, a holster and cleaning kits."

"You wait right here and I will locate the items you need. You can talk to your guide."

Bolan watched as the man hurried from the tunnel. He then turned his attention to the woman. "What's your name?"

"Rachel Jamison."

14

Colonel Diem was startled from his sleep by someone pounding on the door of his hootch. For a moment he didn't know where he was or what he'd been doing, the dreams that had tormented him had been so real. He'd been back in the war, crawling through the jungle in search of targets. Or he'd been fighting for his life as the Americans used him as a target.

He was soaked in sweat. His hair was stuck to his skull, and his breathing was rapid, as if he had just run a long distance. Diem sat up, his bare feet on the wooden floor as his heart hammered. It was the first nightmare he'd had in years, and it had caught him off guard.

The banging at the door continued. "A minute," he shouted, tumbling to the alcove off to the side. He poured himself a glass of water, drank some, then threw the rest over his head and moved toward the door. The OD-green towel he picked up had been taken from a huge stock of supplies left at Cu Chi when the Americans had abandoned South Vietnam.

Diem opened the door and walked back to his cot, followed by one of his lieutenants.

"I have received a message for you, Comrade."

The colonel waved a hand. "Give it to me."

"From our sources in Bangkok, there is word that the next American is preparing for his trip."

Diem was staring at the floor, head bowed, rubbing the back of his neck. "How soon?"

"Our agent wasn't sure, but the indication was that he would begin the trip sometime this morning. With luck, the man might reach our borders sometime about dawn tomorrow."

"Thank you for the information."

The man turned on his heel and left. When he was gone, Diem got up and went back to the sink to clean up. Then he put on his uniform, dressing slowly. There was no chance that the man who was coming could be the Executioner. Diem knew that, and yet he believed that it was going to be the Executioner—an irrational belief based on no evidence other than the bizarre dreams that had tormented him throughout the night.

As he walked through his outer office, he stopped at the wall and studied the wanted poster. The sketched face wasn't quite right, but Diem didn't know exactly what was wrong with it. He'd seen the American sniper through his own scope once or twice, and he had haunted the jungle outside the Executioner's camp, watching for him with binoculars.

He left the hootch and walked slowly to the cage that held Ryan. The prisoner was lying on the floor, the blood from the wounds staining the wood. His face and chest were a mass of purple bruises, and dried blood caked his skin and hair. The bandages on his wounds were filthy. The man was groaning quietly and from the look of him, Diem didn't expect him to live much longer. Not that it mattered now.

Diem crouched, staring at Ryan until the man opened an eye.

"Your replacement is on his way," Diem announced.

Ryan struggled to sit up but couldn't manage it. He fell back onto the floor and drew up his knees, wrapping his arms around his belly. He didn't speak.

"If his job is to find you, then there is hope. If it is to complete the mission you failed, then there is none. You will be left here for us to either let live or to kill."

Still there was no response from Ryan. Diem grinned. "But really, there is no hope. We can capture him the instant it is most convenient for us."

For a moment he stood looking down at Ryan. This man was too young to have fought in Vietnam. He was a youngster who might have watched the war on television or read about it in the newspaper. Yet he was a casualty of that war. It was unfortunate that he wouldn't live much longer, but Diem wasn't in the business of saving the lives of the sick and wounded. If a man couldn't heal himself, he died and was buried in the rice paddies where his remains would do some good fertilizing the next rice crop.

Diem turned and left the cage. He stood in the bright morning sun, watching as the other prisoners were led through the daily ritual. First there was food in the mess hall, a bowl of rice before they moved into the fields to tend the crops that Ryan's body would soon be fertilizing.

He returned to his hootch and sat behind the desk, understanding his nightmares. It was the wine. He'd had more of it than he had thought, emptying the bottle before he had staggered to his cot.

And now the Executioner was on the way. It was a feeling in his gut. No evidence, just a feeling. They would finally finish the battle that had started so long ago. Diem would pay him back for the wounds he'd received the day they'd come face-to-face.

BOLAN WOKE long before Rachel Jamison. He'd given her the bed, then ignored her as she'd stripped. Once she'd appeared in the tunnels owned by the gun merchant, he'd said that she couldn't leave his sight. He hadn't wanted to give her an opportunity to alert anyone about his presence in Thailand. But the merchant had conspired against him, and she'd been missing for almost five full minutes. More than long enough to pass information to anyone who might have been interested.

As Bolan sat cleaning the Remington, Jamison woke and sat up. She swung her feet onto the floor and stretched, giving Bolan a good view of her naked body. He ignored her. Some women assumed that a view of them nude was enough to cancel a man's intelligence. Once he saw a woman without clothes, he would be able to concentrate on nothing else. Bolan turned away pointedly.

Following a loud mock sigh, Jamison abandoned the game and got out of bed. She pulled on her panties and stood in front of the window, staring down into the streets.

"First we need to find a vehicle to get us to the border," Bolan said.

"I will arrange all that. You have the money, and I can find the transportation."

Bolan pulled his chair closer to the table where he'd spread out his map of Southeast Asia. He studied it. "We'll want to cross the border about dusk. With luck we can make the run in the dark and be in position early tomorrow."

"Then we have plenty of time. There is no need to rush."

"Why don't you finish getting dressed so that we can get moving?" Bolan suggested. "We don't have a lot of time to waste."

She pouted for a moment, then picked up her blouse and slipped it over her shoulders. "We could eat here. Call for room service."

"Good idea. While I do that, you can finish dressing."

He turned his back on her, wondering who had planted her on him. She was so obvious that it was ridiculous. He'd have to be really green to fall for her routine. His best course of action was to keep her off balance by not responding to her overtures, and to keep them on the move so that her friends would have a hard time following them.

What he didn't like was the apparent ease the opposition had had in locating him. He'd been in Thailand for about twenty-four hours and already someone had planted a woman on him. It meant that there was a leak somewhere, and that the pipeline from Hal Brognola in Washington wasn't all that tight, either. When he returned, he'd have to pass that information along, and let the boys at Langley figure out who was leaking information.

He made the call to room service, and Rachel Jamison disappeared into the bathroom, closing the door behind her. A moment later the water in the bathtub began to run, and Bolan wondered how soon it would be before she called for him to wash her back.

When the call came, he ignored it, making her shout to him. He sat there, staring at the bathroom door, and in seconds it was opened. She stood framed in the doorway, water dripping onto the floor, glistening on her, highlighting her breasts, hips and thighs. It was a tantalizing picture, but Bolan ignored that, too.

Without a word, she turned, shut the door slowly, carefully, and it was nearly a half hour later before she returned, fully dressed. The blouse was buttoned to the throat, and the short skirt was pulled down so that it covered as much of her legs as possible. Now she'd decided to challenge him with the ice-maiden routine. She would ignore his advances, make him work for any display of affection on her part.

As she sat down, tugging at the hem of her skirt, there was a knock on the door. Room service had arrived.

After the waiter had spread the food on the table and departed, Bolan asked, "How do we go about securing a vehicle?"

"That will be no problem. I know a place to buy one, along with the various licenses and registrations we'll need."

Her response told him she'd be civil, working with him. He would just have to watch her closely until he could get rid of her. But if he cut her loose, he'd have to make sure she couldn't hurt him with her knowledge.

They ate in silence, Jamison keeping her eyes on her plate, pretending to be shy. After the display of the night before and this morning, the act wasn't very convincing. Bolan found it amusing.

When they finished, Bolan gathered his gear, checking the room to make sure he'd forgotten nothing. They left, but rather than going down to the lobby, Bolan and his companion went up to the roof, where they crossed to another building and used the stairs down. They exited on a side street, away from the main entrance to the hotel so that anyone watching the front wouldn't see them leave. He didn't know if anyone *was* there, but there was no reason to make it easy for them.

Jamison led him through the streets until she came to an alley, dragging Bolan behind her. She knocked on a door and waited until someone opened a peephole. The main door opened, and Jamison entered, followed by Bolan.

They were led to a small room that was empty except for a table and four chairs, and were directed to sit there and wait.

Ten minutes later they were joined by a Thai who gave them a once-over and sat down. "What can I do for you?"

Jamison explained their need, and after prolonged haggling over the vehicle, which was described but not seen, they settled on a price. Bolan paid for it, and they were taken through the alley until they came to another door, which led into a warehouse loaded with all sorts of matériel, including several jeeps. The man showed Bolan the one he'd bought, started the engine to show that it worked, then drove it to a huge overhead door.

With Bolan behind the wheel, they left Bangkok, heading northeast. The paved roads soon gave way to bone-jarring ruts and potholes, which slowed their progress considerably. They passed through small hamlets, some of them with stone walls along the road, which looked like English country lanes. In others, there were only mud huts and animals running wild.

Out in the country, where the road was sometimes straight and always narrow, the Thai traffic pushed at him, forcing him to drive faster. Once, a car in the oncoming traffic pulled out to pass a huge truck and didn't make it. The driver jammed on his brakes and slid into the ditch in a cloud of blue smoke caused by the burning rubber. No one stopped as the man leaped from the car, shaking his fist at everyone around him.

They left the farming environment. The houses, up on bamboo stilts, became fewer until the road curved into the looming jungle. Very quickly the road narrowed even more until it looked like a path through a small green tunnel.

Now that they were on the threshold of the jungle, Bolan slowed and pulled over to examine the map. He studied it carefully and realized he was still a good fifty or sixty miles from the Cambodian border. From the map, it looked to be jungle the whole way.

Just as he wondered if there would be much traffic on the road, he heard the low rumble of a diesel. Moments later a converted Army deuce-and-a-half appeared. It was large enough that it straddled the road, the rotting canvas cover over the truck bed touching the vegetation on both sides. It was belching thick clouds of black smoke, and Bolan thought the engine would probably explode within the hour.

As the truck vanished from sight, Bolan pulled back onto the road, holding down his speed because he didn't want to get too close to the border too early. At noon he found a place to stop and eat the little bit of food he'd brought with him. He shared it with Jamison, who didn't seem to care about it one way or the other. They sat listening to the jungle sounds: buzzing insects, animal cries, the occasional swishes in the undergrowth. Their eyes were drawn to a flicker of movement—a lizard running up the trunk of a fallen tree.

A half hour later he started the engine, and they resumed their journey, maintaining a slow pace. At midafternoon they heard a thunderstorm break over the jungle, but the rain didn't penetrate the thick green canopy. There was a sound not unlike frying bacon everywhere that drowned out all other noise. When it stopped, the jungle began to drip as the rain worked its way through the vegetation, sliding down the trunks of the trees, filling the bowl-shaped leaves to tip over splashing water onto the jungle floor in loud, surprising and frightening crashes.

And then they were out of that area. Both had been soaked by the water. Jamison's blouse clung to her skin, nearly transparent until it dried. Bolan didn't look as she struggled to cover the breasts she'd been displaying only a few hours before.

At dusk they stopped for a few minutes. According to the map, they were close to the border. Bolan climbed out of the jeep and walked to the top of the ridgeline, using his binoculars to survey the ground in

front of him. The jungle faded along the border.
Someone had cut it back on either side, making the
border a physical mark on the ground. In the center of
the band, which stretched in either direction as far as
he could see, was a white guard shack that looked deserted. The broken remains of a barricade lay in heaps
across the road.

Bolan crouched at the edge of the jungle and looked
for signs of a trap. After the American withdrawal
from Southeast Asia, Cambodia had been the site of
a bloodbath. As many as two million may have died,
and thousands had fled during the bloody purges of
Pol Pot, who was later overthrown by the Vietnamese.

Since then there had been firefights between Pol
Pot's Khmer Rouge rebels and the Thai army, fights
in both Cambodia and Thailand. But in recent years
things had quieted somewhat as the people who re-
belled against the Vietnamese puppet government were
either killed or fled.

Even so, the border should have been guarded, since
the Khmer Rouge and other guerrilla groups still controlled parts of the country. The government in
Phnom Penh certainly had the means and the man-
power to police the frontier. Yet there was no sign that
anyone was watching, or that anyone had for a number of months, maybe years.

Bolan wrapped the neck strap around his binoculars and headed back to his jeep. He found Jamison
sitting there quietly, spraying herself with insect repellent as the mosquitoes and blood-sucking flies began to swarm.

"I don't like this. The border is too open."

"They don't care anymore," Jamison replied. "If
the malcontents want to flee for the better life in the

West, the Communists couldn't be happier. It leaves only those dedicated to the cause.''

That made a certain amount of sense until the population became so thin that nothing could be done. Then the government would discover that it needed the peasants to do the work. Not everyone could sit in offices making decisions.

And, Bolan realized, there wouldn't be a large number of people trying to sneak into Cambodia. Why would anyone try? Given that, and a possible breakdown of control, meaning that some of the outlying districts would be ignored, the deserted guard shack told him that the trip across Cambodia might be easier than he'd thought. Wait until it was good and dark, then make a run for it. With luck they wouldn't run into government forces, and any patrols they encountered would be very small, not inclined to give chase.

"Let's get a little rest," Bolan said. "It's going to be a long, interesting night."

Jamison stared at him but said nothing. Bolan shrugged. It was going to be more interesting than he had thought.

RYAN FORCED HIMSELF to sit up and crawl to the bucket of water near the door. His jailers had put it there, refusing to bring it closer, as if afraid he would attack them. He knew it was just another of their cruel tricks. If he wanted water, he would have to get it for himself.

Slowly he dragged his broken, damaged body across the rough wooden floor. Each movement was a new adventure in pain. He now had broken ribs and suspected that a lung was damaged. All the fingers on his left hand were broken and swollen to twice their normal size. One ankle was broken, and he thought his lower right leg was also broken. The beatings had left him in constant pain that seemed to grow as he breathed.

Finally he reached the bucket, but was too tired to do anything about it. He lay on the floor, the sweat dripping from him, his breathing labored as he thought about the water only inches from him. The waves of pain washing over him threatened to knock him out. He gritted his teeth, trying to put the pain out of his mind, to somehow separate it from his body so that he could sit up. Then he tried to focus his mind on the water and how good it would taste. Cool water to wash the dirt and blood from his throat. Water that could refresh him and make his life a little more bearable.

With a force of will he wouldn't have believed he possessed, he sat up. His muscles screamed and his nerves shrieked as the pain turned the world red, then white and finally threatened to blacken it completely. He stopped moving, sitting over the water, staring down into the bucket. There was water in it, but not much. He'd have to lower his head to get his drink, but it would be worth the effort.

The knowledge that someone was coming was enough to keep him alive. Since he had been brought into the camp, he hadn't had the chance to see or hear much, but there was one thing he had learned that was vital. One thing that he had to tell the new man because it would change the nature of the whole mission. Just one thing.

He lowered his head into the bucket, and his lips were inches from the water when he saw the floating black shape—a dead mouse hugging the side of the bucket. Ryan's eyes were only an inch from the wet, stinking body, but he didn't care. He squeezed his eyes shut, ignoring the evil trick played on him by his captors in an attempt to deny him the water he so desperately needed. He wouldn't deny himself no matter what was in the bucket.

He tasted the water, drank deeply, feeling it fill him. It slid down his throat and pooled in his belly like a glowing halo of medicine. The relief was almost instantaneous. When he could drink no more, he rocked back. For ten minutes he sat there, letting the water work its magic. Then he worked his way across the floor to his cot, pulling himself up so that he could rest on it.

Someone was on the way. The destination had to be the same as his. Two reasons. One was to search for the Americans who had disappeared in the war and the other to find him. To learn what he knew. If he could get into the field, he could save the man a lot of effort, but that was impossible. He'd have to wait and see if the man made it into the camp. Then Ryan could tell him what he knew.

From outside there was a shout, then silence again. The men who worked in the rice paddies and fields were returning for the evening. They would be given some food. Ryan hoped that someone would come to help him eat. He hoped someone would bring him food. Not that it mattered now. The whole ordeal was nearly over. A day or two longer and nothing would matter anymore.

But Ryan knew he would survive those two days, if the Vietnamese didn't kill him. That was the trick now—surviving the Vietnamese tortures and beatings so that he could pass along his information.

15

At dusk Diem stood in front of his security squad and felt as if he'd been transported back in time. It was the height of the war, and he was going out in search of Americans, or in this case, one American.

His men were dressed in black pajamas or in khaki, and although most of them carried AK-74s, the difference between the older weapon and the newer didn't substantially change the appearance of the rifles. Diem's old Mosin-Nagant was long gone, but he now had one of the Soviet-made Dragunovs. It was a semiautomatic that had been designed for sniping. The one he held had been a gift given to him at the end of the war as a reward for his service. He'd only fired it on the range and once during an elephant hunt in the Central Highlands, which hadn't been much sport.

Because they were operating almost within sight of their camp and didn't plan to be out more than a day or so, they didn't take much in the way of supplies. Each man had a canteen with water and a ration of rice and fish heads. Diem had insisted on that in his attempt to relive his glory days during the war.

At the gate he inspected his men, making them tie down loose equipment, leave their wallets in their hootches, split up the extra ammo. And he made sure that each rifle was clean. He drilled them on the operation so that everyone understood not only his role in the mission, but that of the other men. When Diem found the American, he wanted no mistakes. They would take the man alive so that they could question him.

He checked with the radio operator, making sure that the set worked and that he had spare batteries for it. The last thing he wanted was to get into the field and lose contact with his base. They would be forwarding information on the American's progress. Diem didn't want him slipping through unnoticed because of a radio failure.

Satisfied that the youngsters he'd been given understood their combat mission, he led them through the gate of the camp and out into the open fields. They passed the rice paddies where the white prisoners worked, and came to the jungle where they had found Ryan. Diem began to place his men in such a way that each soldier could see only the man on either side of him. That way Diem had a chain of soldiers scattered through the trees who would be in a position to spot the American.

Once he had completed his instructions, Diem began searching for a place to hide himself. He wandered through the jungle, finding and then rejecting place after place. The foliage was too thick, the ground wasn't high enough, the foliage was too thin, it was too close to the highway, it was too wet. He didn't remember having this much trouble during the war. He had found a spot quickly, almost naturally. Maybe he was rusty, or maybe he hadn't been as concerned about his own comfort then.

Finally he took the high ground, even though the vegetation was thicker than he would have liked. If the enemy crawled into position slowly enough, Diem might miss the movement. But then that was what the other men were for.

As he settled in, the radio operator moved closer and crouched near him. He said, his voice sounding unnaturally loud in the stillness of the jungle, "I have received word that the target has crossed the border into Kampuchea. He has taken the northern route from Sisophon so that he will be avoiding Phnom Penh. It will take him six or seven hours to reach our border."

"You don't need to speak so loudly."

"There is no one around to hear."

Diem shook his head. In the old days a man who spoke back would find himself carrying mortar shells along the Ho Chi Minh Trail. The men in those days understood the necessity of quiet in the jungle, even when the enemy was known to be several hundred kilometers away.

"We will observe noise discipline," Diem ordered. "We will not be caught by surprise. We will remain alert."

"Yes, Comrade Colonel," the radio operator replied.

"Now, you will keep me informed as to our target's progress. When he reaches our border, we will spread the word to all the men."

"Yes, Comrade."

As the man moved off, taking a position to the rear of his colonel, Diem relaxed. This was what he'd been waiting for. He had waited years, dreaming of the day he could get back into the field, searching for the enemy. Now he would capture the invader, unless there was no way to take him alive. Then he would use his weapon and kill the man from a thousand meters, just as he used to do it.

Diem was exhilarated. It was almost impossible to sit still while he waited for the quarry to enter the killing zone. He might have to move from the area, depending on what the others saw and reported, but that would be fine. Diem was prepared to shift the killing ground all over this portion of Vietnam if he had to.

The important point was that by tomorrow the invader would either be dead or he would be captured, singing the songs that Diem wanted to hear. Again Diem would be the darling of the party, with the stories of his greatness circulated at the political meetings held throughout Vietnam.

Tomorrow.

BOLAN WAS UNCOMFORTABLE—it was too easy. If the gods gave you a number of breaks—and the mission was sliding along as if the skids had been greased—he knew a problem was about to loom out of the darkness. Something was about to go wrong.

There was no traffic on the highway. Occasionally, off to one side of the road or the other, he would see lights, fires or lanterns, flickering through the thick jungle vegetation. The towns were as dark and deserted as the ruins at Angkor. Bolan didn't slow down. Instead, he roared through the towns.

Once or twice he thought he caught glimpses of people behind half-drawn shutters, or sitting in dark-

ened buildings, but he wasn't sure. These were merely
fleeting images of human shapes in the dark.

He turned his attention to the woman beside him.
She sat hunched over, as if her stomach hurt, grip-
ping the handle on the dashboard of the jeep, trying
to keep her head out of the wind. The roar made conversation difficult, but Bolan didn't really want to talk
to her anyway.

He still hadn't figured out Rachel Jamison's role in
all this. She seemed to have the contacts he needed,
and she knew her way around Southeast Asia. But like
everything about this trip, his acquisition of her ser-
vices had been too easy. She almost had to be a spy,
though he couldn't see the value she had now. In the
city, where radio signals could be picked up easily, and
she could pass on information with little trouble, she
would be an asset. But out here, in the middle of the
Cambodian jungle, all that was negated. Now she was
just along for the ride.

As he continued to drive through Cambodia, he
thought about his mission. Find out if Americans were
being held in Vietnam. Find out what happened to the
man who had preceded him. But the Executioner had
his own mission, which was the real reason he'd allowed himself to be talked into returning to Vietnam.

At midnight they came to an area where the jungle
gave way to rice fields. The road was a high place
across the paddies. Bolan pulled to the side of the
highway and stopped the jeep. For a moment he sat
there quietly, letting his ears adjust to the silence
around him.

"Why did we stop?" Rachel asked.

"We stopped so that I could stretch my legs. We stopped so that I could walk around for a few minutes."

"This is dangerous," she warned him. "The Communists are all around."

"Nobody's around." Bolan turned slowly in a circle, studying the landscape. No signs of life anywhere. No lights, and no sounds other than the night creatures. There was an odor in the air, not a smell of the tropics, or of the sea, but of death. A lot of people had died in the area.

He walked to the rear of the jeep and leaned against a fender. With his arms folded across his chest, he watched the road behind him, studied it carefully, waiting for some sign that he was being followed. But there was none. No lights on the road, visible for a couple of miles, and no lights in the surrounding fields. There are no aircraft overhead. The country was as deserted and as empty of human signs as it had been at the dawn of time. A sky ablaze with stars, a moon reaching for the zenith, and open ground.

Bolan returned to the driver's seat, climbed in and started the engine. Before he dropped the vehicle into gear, Rachel Jamison reached out and put a hand on his arm. "What's the plan for tomorrow?"

"Haven't thought that far ahead," Bolan said. "Thought I'd play it by ear once I got a look at the lay of the land."

He shifted into first and pulled onto the roadway. As he worked through the gears, he knew exactly what his plan was. Get into a position to observe the camp and wait until the commander showed himself. The instant he did, Bolan would shoot him, and a debt as old as his first tour in Vietnam would be paid in full.

Tomorrow Bolan would have the opportunity of shooting the Rifleman.

DIEM CROUCHED on the high ground overlooking Highway One where it entered the town of Trang Bang. The town had once contained a small market, a soccer field and two or three thousand inhabitants. Now, for the most part, the village was deserted, its mud buildings slowly washing away during the monsoon rains. The rice paddies were overgrown, and the swamp that had been situated to the south was much closer. The landscape was changing slowly now that the people had moved to other places.

But this was the perfect place for Diem. If the American stayed on course—and there were no indications that he would change directions now—he would drive down the highway within a few hours.

The reports from the field, from Siem Reap, Kompong Thom and Tang Krasang, had been positive. The men stationed on the tops of buildings, or hidden along the road, had reported that the jeep had passed them. Two passengers, one man and one woman. There had been no hesitation by the driver. He had hurried through each town and continued on.

Diem relaxed as the last report came in. The enemy was on schedule and on route. It would be another two or three hours before they could expect him.

The colonel closed his eyes for a moment and in his mind saw the wanted poster again: the American known as The Executioner, a sniper who had killed a dozen, two dozen high-ranking VC and NVA offi-

cers, a man who had killed a couple of political officers and who had killed Diem's friend.

Diem remembered the day the Executioner had shot
him. They had just entered a small village. The security team was searching for signs of the enemy and
were hauling out huge bags of rice provided by the
Americans. The villagers who could be found were
herded into the center of the hamlet.

Then he was surprised by the sudden, searing pain
in his shoulder. There was a moment of confusion and
shock before he realized he'd been shot. He had no
idea where the sniper was hidden and could only
scramble for cover, hoping that he'd guessed right and
wasn't exposing himself to the enemy.

Somehow he had survived. Maybe it was because
several men of the security team had sacrificed themselves so that he could get away. Or maybe one or two
of the rounds he'd managed to fire in return had done
some damage to the enemy. He didn't know why he
was able to get out, and it wasn't until months later
that he found out it had been the Executioner who had
been shooting at him.

Diem owed that man for more than just the death
of his friend—he owed him for the wounds he'd received. It was a gift that he became painfully aware of
during the wet season and during days when he was
tired. He planned to even the score in the next few
hours.

Reluctantly he reminded himself that he didn't
know that the man who was coming *was* the Executioner. It could be anyone. But there was that gut
feeling, a perception on a level that Diem didn't understand that told him it was the Executioner. Diem

had learned during his years in the field, stalking Americans, that his gut feelings were more often right than not.

The Rifleman stood, then moved around his blind. It was something he'd ordered the men not to do once they were in place. They had to remain frozen, even knowing that their target was still a hundred miles away. They were not to move. Diem was treating this as if it were a mission during the war, teaching the men the techniques he'd learned in combat.

But he couldn't remain still. He knew that in a couple of hours he would be facing the Executioner, and although he wanted the man alive, he knew that wouldn't happen. By noon one of them would be dead. It was the only way for this to end—in fire, blood and death.

JUST OUTSIDE PHUM KREK Bolan stopped again. He filled the jeep's tank with the gas in the can that had been stored in the rear of the vehicle. Then he walked to the front of the jeep and looked down at the countryside spread out below him.

The words "too easy" kept pounding at him. It had all been too easy. No one had challenged them at the borders; they had encountered no one on the roads. It seemed as if the way had been cleared for them, and that spelled a trap.

Bolan leaned over and retrieved the binoculars from the rear of the jeep, and studied the border between Cambodia and Vietnam. Unlike the last frontier he had crossed, there was no marking between the two countries. As he drove down the highway, he would cross into Vietnam without being aware of it.

He stood there, letting his binoculars roam over the jungle. Again he could see nothing below him, only darkened countryside that had remained unchanged now that the war was over.

If he stayed on the highway, he would pass through Tay Ninh, Go Dau Ha and Trang Bang until he finally came to Saigon. Tay Ninh had been a city of about a million people at the height of the Vietnam War. There had been a sizable Catholic population in the city, and a Cao Dai temple that possessed gold statues worth about a million dollars. A large American camp had stood on the outskirts of the city.

The last thing he needed was to drive along that road. He'd have to merge with the traffic, and he'd be as noticeable as an Oriental driving through the American Midwest. Probably more so now that thousands of Asians had moved into that region.

"We go now?" Rachel asked.

"We *think* now."

She climbed from her seat and stood next to him, forgetting for a moment that she was the ice-maiden. She leaned her head against his shoulder and pressed her hip against his. Then she remembered. She stiffened and moved away.

"This smells like a trap."

"How could they know to set up a trap?" she asked.

"That's a very good question," Bolan returned, "and I don't have a good answer. But this is going too easily for my liking. No one has challenged us so far, and that tells me that the way has been cleared."

"Maybe there are too few people left. Maybe they are only in the big town."

"Yeah," Bolan said, but he didn't believe it. He pulled the map from the back and used his penlight to study it, shielding the beam with his fingers. Not something he would do if he was in a combat environment.

The map told him that there was one main road into the area, but that there were dozens of secondary and country roads, and paths that had been blazed by the Americans that might still exist. One of the reasons he had taken the jeep was that it allowed him to use roads that might not have been in good repair. The four-wheel-drive capability would allow him to use a path that would have stopped a passenger car, and he could drive cross-country if he had to.

Studying the map carefully, Bolan realized there was more than one way to get into the area he wanted. It would be slow progress, but he could avoid the population centers and come up on the prisoner camp from another direction. Once he was in the general area, he could travel through the bush. The ground was solid, and there wasn't much in the way of jungle—light woods that he could negotiate if he worked at it. He might have to backtrack several times, but it wouldn't be a route the enemy expected him to use.

"Back in the jeep," he said to Rachel. "We're on our way now."

Again he started off, moving slowly, watching for signs that someone was following, but he knew that radio stations along his route could have reported his progress. No one had to follow because there weren't that many routes across Cambodia. He realized that he had lulled the Communists into a false sense of security; he had used the route they expected. Now that he was about to divert from it, he would catch them off guard. While they tried to locate him, he would be moving toward his destination.

He drove out of the hills and onto a highway that wasn't marked on his map. It was a wide, dark road, hidden in the trees, peppered with a few potholes and paved in pea gravel. He stopped in the center of it and stared in amazement, realizing that it was a section of the Ho Chi Minh Trail.

Bolan got out of the jeep and crouched so that he could examine the road. Most people had heard of the Trail and assumed it was a narrow pathway through the jungle, but this was as wide as the highways at home. The surface was solid. The vegetation had reclaimed some of the roadway, and the canopy overhead was thick and interwoven, hiding it from the air. It explained why the flow of equipment, supplies and men from the North couldn't be completely stopped.

Standing, he could see that the Ho Chi Minh Trail should have been named the Ho Chi Minh Highway because it wasn't a jungle trail. It was a highway that led into what had been South Vietnam. And he realized that if he was driving into a trap, the Vietnamese wouldn't expect him along the trail. They could cover the main road and some of the secondary highways, but no one would expect him to drive along the Ho Chi Minh Trail. It was ironic. He would be using it to infiltrate the South now.

Bolan returned to the jeep, backed up and turned the wheel. He started down the Trail, driving slowly at first, but even after all these years the road was in very good condition.

"What are you doing?" Rachel asked.

"Sneaking into Vietnam."

"But we've got to stay on the highway. If we stray from it, we'll get lost."

"That I doubt. Temporarily disoriented, but not lost. All I have to remember is to keep heading more or less to the east, and we'll get to where we want to go."

"You can't do that," she protested.

Bolan stopped the jeep and faced her. "And why can't I do that?"

She shrugged helplessly. "This road will vanish, and we'll be stuck in the jungle."

"Then we'll turn around and drive back this way. There's no timetable."

"The sun will be up soon."

"We'll sleep through the day if we have to. There's no hurry."

Again she started to speak but stopped abruptly, realizing she could protest too much.

Bolan waited, but Rachel didn't say another word. He dropped the jeep into gear and rolled forward, turning on the headlights since the thick canopy now blocked the stars and the moon. He sped up, dodging the bigger potholes and bouncing through the others.

They continued southeast. The Trail crossed a number of small streams and the Prek Tate, using underwater bridges that had been built during the Vietnam War. These were shallow places in the water, built up by the Vietcong so that enemy planes wouldn't be able to spot them. It was an effective device that hadn't eroded during the years.

They progressed along the Trail, stayed on the Cambodian side of the border, skirting Vietnam. They passed far to the west of Tay Ninh, then worked their way south, entering the area the GIs had called the Angel's Wing. When the Trail crossed a small road that had once been paved, Bolan turned onto it. He would be able to drive south of Go Dau Ha and stay south of Highway One until he reached Trang Bang. Then he'd have to find a road that would take him around to the east side of town.

He stopped once and considered putting Rachel out of the jeep. It would take her hours to find help, and probably a day or more to find a way to communicate with the Vietnamese government. But he decided he couldn't take the risk. She might be able to blow the whistle on him in an hour, and he didn't want to alert the enemy that he was so close.

He checked the map and then took off. Rachel Jamison sat beside him stiffly, looking frightened. She no longer talked to him. It was as if he had violated some rule, and she was punishing him for it. He didn't mind because he needed to concentrate on his driving.

There was still more than an hour to dawn when he passed south of the darkened and silent Trang Bang. He found an old road that took him north toward Trung Lap and the Hobo Woods. Fifteen minutes later he parked the jeep in a grove of palm and coconut trees. After he shut off the engine, they were cloaked in silence.

Bolan climbed out of the jeep and reached into the back for his rifle. He opened the case and examined his weapon carefully, finding no evidence that it had been damaged during the trip. Then, without speaking to Jamison, he began to get ready to move through the woods.

"What am I supposed to do?" she asked.

Bolan looked at her, little more than a dark shape in the night, and said, "That's a very good question." It was one that he hadn't been thinking about because he knew what the right answer would have been. A cold, callous man would kill her. That way she would be in no position to cause him trouble. She wouldn't pop up at the worst possible moment or shout a warning to the enemy.

He could tie her up and leave her in the jeep, but that might be a death sentence. The tropical sun would dehydrate her quickly, and if something happened so that he couldn't get back to her, she would die if no one found her.

The only thing to do was to take her with him. He couldn't trust her, but she had done nothing to him yet. If there were traps laid, he had avoided them. She had helped, after a fashion, directing him to the place to buy his jeep and suggesting the best routes to get here.

"We'll head through the woods," Bolan said. "You have to be absolutely quiet. No noise at all."

"I'll do my best."

Bolan walked around the jeep and looked at her clothes. A light blouse and short skirt weren't the proper garb for the jungle, but there was nothing he could do about it. She would be lost in his clothes. They would be too large for her.

He handed her a canteen and said, "This is your water. When you've finished it, you'll get no more. I won't share mine with you, so keep that in mind."

She nodded but didn't speak.

"If you cause me trouble, I'll tie you up and leave you. No second chances."

Again she nodded.

A final check of his gear and he was ready. Bolan shouldered his pack and picked up his rifle. He pointed at Jamison and said, "Stay close and no noise."

They moved through the jungle easily. Bolan wasn't sure the area could be called jungle because it was so light—stunted trees and scraggly bushes. There was knee-high grass and clumps of taller trees, but not the thick growth that was associated with a rain forest. The bright glow from the moon and stars provided enough light for them to negotiate the terrain. They stayed close to the tree line, using the shadows to hide their silhouettes.

Although it was night, there was still humidity in the air, and Bolan found himself sweating heavily. He wiped at his forehead with the sleeve of his shirt and kept the pace slow, moving ever closer to the enemy camp.

They kept going in dogged silence for nearly half an hour. Jamison made no attempt to conceal her movements. She stomped through the forest as if her feet were huge, but Bolan didn't mind. This wasn't the war, where there would be ambush patrols scattered all over the countryside. This was a peaceful environment where farmers would have to get to their fields early in the morning. People walking through the bush at this hour would be an everyday occurrence.

Then Bolan dropped to one knee. They had come to the edge of the trees and were looking out over open ground. Nearly half a kilometer away, outlined by the setting of the moon, was the camp he had traveled halfway around the world to find. There were only a couple of lights visible, and the sounds of a radio—but no other signs of life.

He'd made it. Granted, he was walking into a trap, but not from the direction they expected.

Rachel stood beside him, then stepped into the open. Bolan grabbed her arm and jerked her back. She fell heavily, grunting in surprise.

"Hey!"

"Quiet. We lie low now and watch. That's all we do."

"I'm hungry."

"Then eat. But do it quietly. And if you're tired, you can go to sleep. I think we're going to be here for a while."

She sat up but didn't speak again. Bolan kept his eyes on the camp, wondering if the Rifleman was in his headquarters or his hootch, or if he was spending the night in Saigon. Maybe the Rifleman didn't live at this camp. Maybe he'd just been there on a visit when his picture had been taken. Bolan refused to believe he'd come all this way so that his quarry could slip through his fingers again.

He settled in and scanned the perimeter of the camp with his binoculars. In a couple of hours it would all be over. He hoped to be on his way out of Vietnam by noon. With luck he would have the answers that Brognola and Moore wanted. With a little luck.

16

As the night slowly turned to dawn and the radio operator remained silent, Diem began to worry. There should have been some word on the American. He'd passed through Phum Krek and then vanished. He hadn't crossed the border and hadn't passed through either Tay Ninh or Go Dau Ha, and it was beginning to brighten. He must have gotten lost, or perhaps he had pulled over to rest through the day. He would make his final run in the dark.

Diem crawled back to where the radio operator waited and tapped the man on the shoulder. "Anything yet?"

"Nothing for a long time."

"Is it working?"

"Yes, Comrade Colonel, it is working just fine. They have had nothing to report."

Diem wanted to order the man to contact the people in Kampuchea and ask again about the American, but that would accomplish nothing. The men would radio any information as soon as they got it.

The colonel slipped back into his blind and stared at the black ribbon of highway that wound its way west and north into Kampuchea. Nothing was moving on it. And he remembered one often repeated phrase from the war: to move at night was to invite an ambush.

He settled in and touched the equipment he had set in a pattern in front of him. Extra ammo, an illumination flare, binoculars. His rifle was lying on its leather case, the operating rod up so that it wouldn't drag in the dirt. All he could do was continue to wait for the American. The first move had to be his.

BOLAN HAD EXPECTED the scene below him to change as the sun came up. He'd expected the camp to come alive, but that didn't happen. Instead of activity in the interior, there was no movement whatsoever. If he hadn't known better, he would have thought the camp was deserted.

And then one man came from a hootch, a short man wearing khaki pants and carrying a towel over his shoulder. He entered another hootch. A second man appeared, walked across the compound and vanished. A moment later smoke began to curl from the chimney of one of the hootches.

Slowly the camp came awake. More men began to circulate, some of whom were armed, carrying rifles. And white men appeared. Bolan studied them, tall, thin white men who were being watched by the men with the weapons.

There was something wrong with the scene, though. The men looked to be very old. Bolan knew that some Americans were in their late thirties or early forties when they were shot down and captured. Some men had been captured as early as 1965 or 1966, so those men could be in their sixties. But the men in the camp looked much too old to be Americans captured during the Vietnam War.

Now Bolan had a dozen questions. If these men, moving among the hootches, were too old to have been soldiers in Vietnam, and they couldn't be Americans, then who were they? Maybe it was the captivity and the years of slave labor that made them seem older than their years.

He glanced at Jamison, wondering if she had any of the answers. He could ask her, but then she'd have to admit to working with the Vietnamese if she answered with anything other than an "I don't know." And he had no evidence she was an enemy agent.

Bolan watched the camp for several hours but saw very little. The men didn't move into the fields to work. The guards circulated, staying just inside the wire—too few guards for the number of men Bolan had seen.

And more importantly, the Rifleman hadn't appeared. Bolan had spotted the building he was sure was the headquarters, a small structure with a flagpole in front of it near the main gate. No one went near the HQ, though, and Bolan wondered if the commander was asleep.

As the sun climbed higher, the heat that had been absent earlier returned. Bolan felt the sweat soak through his clothes, and he glanced at Jamison, who was lying at the base of a palm tree, staying in the shade. Her clothes were damp, and her hair hung limply, as though she'd just stepped from the shower. She didn't speak and didn't move.

By noon Bolan was thinking of trying to penetrate the enemy camp. There was good cover from the tree line up to the fence. It was obvious the Vietnamese weren't worried about someone sneaking up on their camp. Considering how lax things looked, Bolan was sure he could make it.

But he remembered the rule that had been drilled into soldiers in Vietnam. The Oriental respected patience. To show impatience was to lose face. Bolan was becoming impatient, and that could cause him to lose much more than face.

He crawled to the rear, away from the edge of the tree line, and sat up. Picking up his canteen, he drank from it, filling his mouth with water and sloshing it around before he swallowed it. What he had to do would be difficult enough. He didn't need to make it worse by drinking all his water at once.

He pulled some of the rations he'd brought from his pack and ate them. He no longer had to worry about the heavy C-ration cans with almost inedible food that they had used in Vietnam. Changes had been made. Freeze-dried food had taken the place of the C-rats. Some of it was terrible, but some of it was fairly good. Most importantly, though, a little was all that had to be eaten. One man could carry a month's supply, along with everything else he needed.

When he finished, he crawled back to the edge of the trees and resumed his surveillance of the camp. The headquarters remained vacant, no one approaching or leaving it. There was no sign of the Rifleman, or the men who would have been assigned to the camp.

Which almost had to prove that it was a trap. Those men were out searching for him. Maybe they were lined up along the highway waiting for his jeep, or standing off, outside the camp, watching for him. Or maybe they were hiding inside the camp, waiting for him to show up.

He retreated into the trees to rest. Sitting with his back against the rough trunk of a palm, he closed his eyes. He would take it easy through the afternoon, moving out with the night, cloaking himself in darkness to cover his approach to the camp.

AT DUSK Bolan moved back to the edge of the jungle and watched what little activity was taking place. A couple of guards made their rounds, and occasionally a white man was shepherded from one hootch to another. No one had used the headquarters hootch all day, and Bolan knew it meant that no one was inside. Something strange was going on in the camp, and the only way to find out what, was to go down and take a look.

But that was a problem. He couldn't leave Rachel Jamison behind because he couldn't trust her. And he couldn't take her with him because the slightest mistake could be fatal for him. She didn't have to do much to warn the enemy, and if she handled it right, he'd never be able to tell whether it was an honest mistake or an actual warning.

Bolan returned to the dense vegetation again and found Rachel sitting on the soft, rotting leaves eating part of a candy bar. She glanced at him, but said nothing.

"We've got to move deeper into the forest," he told her.

She raised her eyebrows in question, but didn't argue. Instead she picked up the candy wrapper and her canteen and stood. She followed Bolan as he worked his way through the trees and bushes until he came to a tree that was a half a meter in diameter and fifty meters tall.

"Sit down here," he told her.

When she complied, he moved behind her and took her wrists in his hands, gently drawing them to the rear.

"Hey! What are you doing?"

"I have to go into the camp, and I'm leaving you here."

She felt the cord bite gently into her wrists. "This is unnecessary," she protested. "You don't have to do this."

"Keep your voice down," Bolan warned.

"I could scream," she said. "I could yell for help, and then where would you be?"

"If you did that, you'd prove my point. Now, if you're quiet, I'll come back to get you later."

"If you leave me, I'll scream."

Bolan pulled a handkerchief from his pocket. "I suspected you'd say that." He reached around and grabbed her jaw, forcing her mouth open. Before she realized what was happening, he stuffed the wadded ball of cloth into her mouth. Using a second piece of cloth, he tied it into place, making an effective gag.

"Now you can try to yell, but it won't do you much good. The sound won't carry far, and you'll only damage your throat. Now be good, and I'll come back to get you."

Rachel began to kick her feet, drumming them on the ground. She twisted and turned, her eyes rolling at him in anger.

"I was afraid of this," he said quietly. Using a length of rope, he tied her ankles together, then looped the end around her right ankle. He drew her legs up so that her knees were pressed against her chest. Looping the rope around the tree, he tied the other end to her left ankle, making it impossible for her to straighten her legs and stand up.

Finished, he stepped away. He looked down at her, regret in his eyes. "I know it's going to be uncomfortable, but it won't be for long. I'll free you as soon as I can."

She grunted at him and strained at the ropes, but couldn't free herself. Sweat popped out on her forehead and dripped down her face.

Bolan left her there and hurried back to the edge of the jungle. He checked his pack, taking those things he was sure he would need—pistol, rifle, combat knife and flashlight. Everything else was unnecessary for what he had to do.

He hesitated at the tree line. For a moment he listened, but could hear nothing unusual. If Jamison was making any noise, it didn't reach him. He was sorry he'd had to leave her like that, but it was better than having to knock her out.

He focused his attention on the camp, but the limited activity of the day had all but vanished. No one was moving. Music drifted on the light breeze, and there was a flickering of candlelight. It seemed that no one down there saw any need for nighttime security.

Since there were no guard movements to time, no changing of the guard to add to the confusion, and very little light coming from the camp, Bolan decided there was no time like the present. He slipped from his

cover, snaking forward quickly. The grass, almost a
meter high, protected him. He moved on his elbows,
belly and knees, using the crawl he had learned in the
Army years before. It was physically demanding,
making the muscles in his arms and legs ache. His
breathing became ragged as he realized that a man in
top condition who wasn't used to this kind of crawl
would find it difficult.

He progressed at a steady pace, getting closer to the
camp. Halfway there he stopped to rest and wished he
had brought his canteen. He could have used a drink
of water. Part of it was psychological and part of it
was actual thirst.

The music he'd heard earlier stopped abruptly as
someone snapped off the radio. There was a single
bark of laughter, then silence. Too bad about the radio, Bolan thought. The music would have covered
any noise he made.

Feeling rested, he started forward again. The wire
that surrounded the camp wasn't the convoluted mess
of concertina and tanglefoot Americans had used
during the war. It was more of a fence to keep the animals out, and not designed to keep the prisoners in.
Bolan crawled under the lowest strand, working his
way closer to the berm. He located one claymore mine,
but it was a rusting hunk of metal without firing con-
trols attached. Behind it was the rotten remains of a
sandbag. Obviously it was a relic from the war.

Bolan worked his way closer to the berm, which was
a dike only a half meter high that ran around the
camp. He rested at its base, listening to the quiet sound
of the voices from the camp—Vietnamese talking to
one another, some French spoken in even quieter

tones, but no English. Bolan knew that some of the
men held by the Vietcong during the war had learned
the Vietnamese language as a matter of survival, but
surely someone would be speaking English.

He peeked over the top of the berm and found that
the camp appeared deserted. No one was moving. He
could make out patches of light and areas of black
shadow, but no movement.

Bolan reached up, pulled himself onto the berm and
slid into the camp. No Klaxons blared, no lights
flashed. He'd penetrated the perimeter unobserved.
The first order of business was to take out the guards
who were around.

Slowly he made his way toward one of the hootches
where the Vietnamese talked. When he reached it, he
slipped into a shadow and slowly stood upright. He
peeked into a window and saw four men playing cards
while two others watched. A seventh man separated
himself from the group and headed for the door. Bolan eased to the rear as a sliver of light flashed.

Growling noisily, the man stepped into the night and
stretched, lifting his arms toward the sky, which blazed
with stars. Then he stepped from the hootch and came
around the corner, his gaze landing on Bolan but apparently not seeing him.

The Executioner attacked swiftly. In one fluid motion he propped his rifle against the hootch, drew his
knife and slashed at the enemy soldier. The man reeled
back in surprise as Bolan grabbed his mouth and nose.
The knife flashed, and a splash of warm blood flowed
over Bolan's hand. The man grunted and slipped to his
knees. The Executioner followed him, keeping his
hand clamped on the Vietnamese's face. His teeth bit

at Bolan's palm, but did no damage; his hands grabbed at Bolan's wrist, but there was no strength in his fingers. As the man's eyes rolled up into his head, the warrior let him fall gently onto the grass.

As that man died, a second left the hootch. He stopped near the door and called, "Ngo? Ngo?"

When there was no answer, he, too, stepped around the corner of the hootch. He spotted the body at once and ran to it. As the second soldier crouched near his dead comrade, the Executioner struck again. From behind, he grabbed the man's chin, jerking it up. The knife bit the soft flesh, ripping through it. A cry died in the man's throat and he spasmed, kicking out as the last of his blood pumped from severed arteries. He died without knowing what had happened to Ngo.

Bolan then rolled the two bodies under the hootch where they would be out of sight. He glanced into the lighted room, but the men there suspected nothing. They continued to play cards and talk to one another.

Bolan moved away from the hootch, part of his attention on the cardplayers, waiting for the shout of alarm. He worked his way toward the headquarters, but before he got there, he checked a darkened hootch. Listening at the door, he could hear the soft breathing of one person. Bolan catfooted toward the door and found that it was barred. He felt around the outside of it, realizing he had located some kind of cage.

From the darkness came a tired, quiet voice. "Who's there?"

"You speak English?" Bolan asked.

"God, yes."

"Who are you?"

"Ryan. Thomas Ryan. I was arrested by these people and brought here."

"I'm here to get you out." Bolan ran his fingers along the cage door, searching for a lock. He found a latch that had no lock and opened it, stepping inside.

"Listen," Ryan said urgently. "You've got to get out of here! I'm no good to you. These other men held here. They're not Americans. They're French."

"What?"

"They're all French, left over from the war. I'm the only American here. You've got to get out and tell Congress about it before they waste anyone else."

Bolan moved across the darkened floor, stopped near the voice and snapped on his flashlight. The face that looked up at him was badly beaten. Dried blood caked the eyes and lips. The nose was flattened and shoved to one side, obviously broken. There was a stench rising from the man—the stench of sickness and death. He was in bad shape.

"You can't do anything for me," Ryan said. "I'm a goner."

"I've got transportation close at hand. I can get you out. But first I have some business to attend to."

"Listen," Ryan rasped, the words coming in a rush now. "They knew you were coming. They're out looking for you. Who knew that you were coming at our end?"

Bolan thought about that. No one really knew. Moore, Brognola and no one else. Neither man would leak the information because neither man was in a position to leak it.

"No one knew."

"Someone had to. Only one man knew I was coming, and they were waiting for me. McDonald in Bangkok. He knew. He had to tell someone."

"Listen," Bolan said, "I've got some business to finish. You wait here and I'll be back."

"Forget me. Get out with the information. Get McDonald, that dumb son of a bitch. Kill him."

"You try to relax, and I'll get you out, too." Bolan snapped off the light.

Ryan put his hand on the Executioner's arm. "I have an emergency route out through Vung Tau. At midnight there's a junk that will take you back to Bangkok."

"You rest. I'll be back." Bolan stood and made his way to the door. Now he wanted to free the French prisoners. He couldn't get them out of Vietnam, so they'd have to do that themselves, but he could give them the chance. And that would confuse the issue, giving him a better chance to escape.

Bolan hesitated at the door, but the Vietnamese still seemed to be unaware that he had penetrated the camp. He dropped to the ground, keeping to the shadows, worked his way deeper into the camp. He found the door to a hootch and listened. The voices were speaking French. Bolan, surprised that the door wasn't locked, opened it and stepped inside. There was a dim light in the corner, and near it were the huddled shapes of the Frenchmen. One man turned and looked at Bolan.

"Do any of you speak English?"

An extremely gaunt man rose slowly and turned, but said nothing.

"Listen, this is your chance. You've got to get out of here now. You'll have a good head start, maybe ten, twelve hours."

"And where would we go?" the man asked, his English heavily accented, almost unintelligible.

"Saigon or Tay Ninh, or to the Michelin Rubber Plantation. The important thing is to get out of here."

"No," the man replied. "It is too late for us. We are too old and too tired and too sick. We can no longer escape."

"As long as you can move, you can escape."

The man shook his head, a slow movement that showed his age. "It is too late. We would all die."

"Isn't it better to die like men than to live like slaves?"

From the darkened corner came a single word. "Yes."

"Then go. I will handle the guards here and slow them down. Free your fellows and get out of here."

"We will do what we can," the voice returned.

"Good!" Bolan whirled and ran from the hootch. He returned to where the guards were playing cards. This time he stepped to the door and kicked it open. He stood there, his Desert Eagle in his hand. As the guards went for their weapons, he opened fire.

The first man took a head shot and was punched back against the wall. The second was shot in the chest, the round punching through the sternum to shatter the bone and the heart. He fell to the floor in a heap, as though his bones had suddenly disintegrated. Another soldier had grabbed his weapon, but Bolan killed him before he could get off a round. The huge slug tore into his throat, nearly ripping his head from his body.

Bolan spun, but the fourth man had jumped through a window. He fired at the last man, and the round hit him in the shoulder. The guy collapsed, then struggled to reach one of the weapons lying on the floor. He didn't make it.

The Executioner ran from the hootch. The guard who'd jumped through the window had gotten away. Bolan didn't care because that wasn't the man he'd come to get. The Rifleman was the target, and if one of the guards ran into the jungle to find the Rifleman, it made Bolan's job that much easier.

He sprinted across the open ground and slid to a halt in front of the HQ hootch. This time he tried the knob, surprised that the door would open. He stepped inside and then crouched, listening, but there was no one in there with him.

Bolan turned on his flashlight and played the beam along a wall covered with photographs. He looked them over, recognizing the Rifleman in a dozen shots. Then he came to the wanted poster with his "old" face on it. He stared at the drawing, a chill running up and down his spine.

The Executioner stepped back and rubbed his face and his hand came away covered with sweat. The significance of finding that poster wasn't lost on him. He hadn't realized the enemy soldier had felt the way he did, hadn't considered the possibility the Rifleman had held a grudge for all these years. It was a strange, frightening thing. A man who was somehow the exact opposite of Bolan. A man who had done the same job during the war, but who had become a twisted despot controlling the lives of men just because they had been the enemy so many years before.

Bolan was caught completely off guard. This wasn't something he had expected. He felt an affinity for the Rifleman he hadn't experienced in the field. It was as if he knew the man personally. The framed wanted poster told Bolan all he needed to know.

And then he realized he was wasting time. He was like an animal caught in a trap, so fascinated by his own image in a mirror that he didn't try to escape. If he stood there long enough, the Rifleman would be able to walk up behind him and kill him.

Bolan quickly searched the rest of the headquarters, moving into the Rifleman's living area. There wasn't much there—a cot, a chair and a few books.

He stepped back into the office and knew the Rifleman wouldn't enter the camp. The Vietnamese sniper would know time was on his side. Patience would be rewarded by Bolan exposing himself, unless Bolan could draw him into the open. That would be the trick.

The Executioner knew the Rifleman would go to the edge of the jungle and wait for him. Bolan's job was to kill him. As he stepped into the clear, cool night, Bolan knew exactly how to do it. The Rifleman had provided the key to the puzzle himself.

Glancing at his watch, Bolan saw that the night was almost over. It had passed quickly. The long crawl through the grass had eaten a great deal of it, but there was plenty of time for Bolan to get ready.

17

Bolan settled in, crouched in the roof of the hootch, a firing port created by his knife. From there he could see the whole west side of the camp from Highway One on the south side, north toward the Saigon River. He was high enough so that the trees and surrounding terrain didn't get in the way.

Around him, in the thick thatch, he could hear the scrambling of tiny claws—lizards and rats that had made their homes there. He ignored the sounds, concentrating on the upcoming task.

It hadn't taken him long. The French had told him that only a few of the guards had been in the camp, and Bolan had already eliminated that threat. The French then scattered, moving east and south. Bolan returned to Ryan. The man was in bad shape, barely able to stand. Bolan broke the chain around his ankle and helped him to the cot. Together they fashioned him a crutch, then the warrior told him to head for the jungle east of the camp, where he'd be able to see Bolan's path through the grass. All he had to do was follow it back and wait for him there. Bolan would join up with him later.

Before he began his journey, Ryan grabbed Bolan's arm. "You'll never be able to escape the way you came. They'll be waiting for you. Use my escape route.''

"All right," Bolan said.

Ryan then gave him the rendezvous information, the passwords and the alternates in case something went wrong. Bolan repeated them and Ryan nodded.

"One other thing. You have to kill Diem." Ryan was seized by a coughing spell that shook his body and forced him to his knees. He wiped his swollen mouth with the back of his hand. "This is stupid. I should just stay here."

"You get out. I'll join you."

"And you'll kill Diem. He thinks he was so smart, pulling that old Mutt and Jeff routine on me. Tell me something and I'll be able to stop the beatings." Ryan tried to grin, but that only twisted his face into a fright mask. "I knew what was happening. I had to stay alive until I could pass along the information. Now you kill him."

"That's why I'm here."

He helped Ryan into the field. As the wounded man began the slow journey toward the jungle, Bolan returned to the camp. He found one of the lanterns and hung it in the window of Diem's hootch. He turned it on and then retreated. He would use it to draw the Rifleman into the open.

Now the Executioner settled into his nest to wait. That was all he had to do. Sit there, sheltered by the thatch, the sun rising behind him, and wait for the enemy to show himself—which would happen when Bolan didn't appear on the road leading to the camp. Couple that with the shooting in the night, and Diem would have to figure something was wrong. He'd wait until daylight before coming back. The light was his friend and Bolan's enemy.

Dawn approached slowly. There was a graying of the sky as the stars began to fade. Birds began to stir, calling to one another, and the jungle animals began to scurry through the undergrowth. Bolan didn't let his attention wander now. He had to concentrate, watch for signs that the enemy was coming.

He didn't have long to wait. As the jungle changed from a black smudge to charcoal, then gray and finally brightened completely, Bolan saw the men moving in the shadows and early-morning mist, light gray shapes that leaped, moved and then disappeared.

He studied each of the approaching men through the scope mounted on his rifle. Sometimes he could see the face well. The mist would thin or the sunlight would flash, and each time Bolan waited to identify his target.

This was the maneuvering before the final show. Diem was trying to draw fire to learn if Bolan was still there, or if he had retreated with the sun. The Rifleman had to know that his camp had been raided and the men left behind dead.

Even with that, no one left the cover of the jungle. They stayed at the edge, half a kilometer away, tempting him with targets he didn't take. He watched and waited, remembered that patience was his ally.

When the sun had climbed high enough so that the ground was no longer enshrouded in shadows and the morning mist had burned off, Bolan shifted to the right. He could see the lantern hanging in the window, still burning brightly. He aimed carefully and squeezed off a single round. The bottom of the lantern exploded, and kerosene splashed over the walls of the hootch, catching fire immediately. Smoke began to pour from the walls and billowed into the thatch, which was slowly beginning to burn.

"Now," Bolan whispered. "Let's see if you'll let your trophies burn."

His one shot was answered by a burst of fire from an AK, which was joined by another and another until there were a dozen weapons pumping rounds into the camp. Bolan surveyed the jungle, and in the shadows could pick out the flickering of muzzle-flashes. A few of the rounds slammed into the thatch near him, kicking up clouds of dust. One snapped by his head as it passed through the hootch. But the shots weren't aimed. The Vietnamese were firing blind, hoping to get lucky.

Bolan waited, and as soon as one of the men stepped into the clearing, he focused the cross hairs on his head. Slowly he began to pull the trigger, then stopped. It wasn't the Rifleman, just some low-ranking soldier ordered to make a target of himself. Bolan didn't take the shot.

More of the Vietnamese walked into the clearing. They began to sweep forward slowly, but still the Rifleman had failed to reveal himself. Bolan knew the guy was crouched in the jungle with a spotter or two, searching for him. They were trying to provoke Bolan into shooting, but he refused to take the bait.

To his right, the headquarters hootch was almost engulfed. The thatch had caught fire, and the smoke and flames were leaping into the air, the dry grass snapping and crackling as it burned.

More of the Vietnamese poured into the clearing, approaching the camp rapidly. Bolan wondered if he should try to stop them, then decided against it. The target was still in hiding, ordering more of his men into the field in an attempt to force Bolan to reveal himself.

Bolan realized his plan had failed. He'd assumed the Rifleman would rush forward to save his few possessions, the reminders of war that had fueled his hate. But he didn't have to do that. He could send his men in. Bolan would have to stop them to force the issue.

The warrior dropped to the floor of the hootch and ran out the back way, sliding to a halt next to the wall of another hootch. He took aim at the man closest to him. Through the scope he could see the man quite well—a young man with a couple days' growth of beard on his face who looked tired and sweaty.

Bolan caressed the trigger, and the rifle fired, dirt flying from the front of the man's uniform as he hit the ground.

The other soldiers kept coming, none of them firing. Bolan fired another round and saw a soldier's head explode into a fine mist of crimson. The headless corpse took one step, then collapsed.

Now Bolan moved. He ducked, ran to the right and found another position. He aimed, fired and didn't wait to see the results. Instead, he ducked back and dropped to the ground. As he crawled under the hootch, the enemy began firing again. The rounds ripped into the camp, slamming into the hootches. Windows shattered and bullets ricocheted. There was a growing shout from the field outside, and the Vietnamese began a surging charge.

Bolan crawled forward. It was difficult to see over the berm. He aimed at one of the Vietnamese and fired. That man collapsed and disappeared. Bolan rolled to the right and reloaded, working the bolt of the Remington. When he looked up, the Vietnamese were closer, firing their AKs from the hip.

They were so close now that the scope was unnecessary, and as he fired, he could see the expressions on their faces, expressions of surprise and pain as the men died. He could see the bullets ripping into the flesh and see the blood as it splattered.

And then the last of the Vietnamese were gone—either in hiding or killed. Bolan slipped to the rear and stood up. He crouch-ran back to the hootch where he'd hidden earlier and climbed into the thatch. He turned his attention on the jungle, searching for the Rifleman.

DIEM WATCHED as the last of his men tumbled to the grass. He knew they weren't dead, but the rifle fire from the camp had been so accurate, so deadly, that for them to remain standing would mean death. There was no way for them to get into the camp now.

Diem used the scope on his rifle to search for the enemy sniper. The sun, behind him, effectively masked the American's muzzle-flashes, and he was apparently moving around. The colonel couldn't spot him.

Then his attention was drawn to the fire in the camp. He knew what was burning—his headquarters with everything he owned, other than the rifle he held and the clothes he wore. Everything else was in that building, including the photographs that were the only things he had left from his earlier life. The smoke rising from the camp was like a knife in his heart.

He stood and watched as the flames spread across the roof. And then he grinned. It was a masterful plan. The Executioner had been in the hootch and seen the photos, had understood their meaning. The man couldn't hold his men hostage, but he could try to draw him out of the jungle by burning the hootch.

But he wouldn't fall for a trick like that. The photos might vanish in the fire, but Diem would remember what they had depicted. He had spent too many hours sitting at his desk staring at them to forget. In his mind he could call up the scene. He could see the arrangement on the wall, and he could move closer, examining each picture individually. A nice try, but it wouldn't work.

Using the scope on his Dragunov sniper rifle, he searched the camp but couldn't spot the Executioner. Now with patience, he would be able to settle the score that was years old.

Turning to the right where the RPD Soviet-made machine gun was positioned, he said, "Open fire. Rake the whole camp."

"Our comrades?"

"If they are still in the camp, they are dead. Let's see if we can find this Executioner."

The machine gun began to thunder. Through his scope, Diem could see the impact of the rounds. Dirt was kicked up into the air; bits of wood splintered from the hootches; the windows shattered. The machine gun seared the camp from one end to the other and back again, but the maneuver drew no response from Bolan.

Diem nodded and grinned. The Executioner was the best he had ever faced, a man who understood much of being a sniper, who understood patience and knew that the first man who made a mistake would be the one to die. His use of the fire had been clever, and his stopping the men sent to put it out even cleverer. He had taken the situation that was heavily stacked against him and turned it to his advantage. Diem wasn't sure that if the situation had been reversed he could have done as well.

He continued to search for the enemy, wondering what he could do to draw him out. There didn't seem to be a way. It was a stalemate, although, if Diem used all his resources, bringing in assistance from outside, he could end it quickly.

That would be the smart thing. Leave a couple of men here to keep the Executioner pinned down and go find help. But then the credit would have to be shared, and Diem didn't want that. He wanted to kill the Executioner by himself. He wanted to capture the man and kill him slowly, making him pay for Tuy and all the Vietnamese who had died at his hands. And for the burning of his hootch.

If he was patient, the advantages would turn to him. The man was alone, hiding in an enemy country. He would have to move soon, or he would be caught and killed.

The RPD fell silent as the men used up the last of the belt. The barrel was extremely hot, and if they kept firing, they would burn it out.

"In a few minutes, open fire again," Diem ordered.

BOLAN LOOKED through his scope, searching the jungle. He spotted the machine gun almost as soon as it opened fire. Among the thick vegetation, he could see the gunner and his assistant as they pumped out rounds. He could take out the gunners if he wanted, but they posed no great danger to him.

Then, through a small gap in the jungle, he saw the foot of another man. He stood, concealed behind a tree. Nothing else showed, just the one foot. Bolan knew it belonged to the Rifleman.

The warrior knew the situation was one that couldn't last. The advantages he had held were soon going to evaporate. The Rifleman could stay in the jungle and pin him down until more men were brought in.

He checked the wind and saw that it was blowing away from him. It wasn't a crosswind, which was a good thing. He put the cross hairs on the foot, aiming at the ankle. He took a deep breath, exhaled and sucked in more air. This was the crucial shot. He had to make it. He exhaled partially, and began to take in the slack on the trigger. He kept pulling at it, waiting for the weapon to fire.

As soon as he made the shot, Bolan worked the bolt. He saw the round strike in an explosion of blood and bone, but for a moment nothing happened. It was as if the Rifleman didn't know he'd been shot.

Then a body crashed into view. Bolan saw the face for the first time since he had returned to Vietnam, a face that was older than he remembered and twisted in pain, but a face he recognized.

Bolan put the cross hairs on Diem's forehead and pulled the trigger. Just as the weapon fired, the eyes of the Rifleman turned toward him, and Bolan felt as if the man were looking right at him. There was recognition in those eyes. The Rifleman knew he had finally faced the one man he had longed to face and had lost.

The round struck, and the face was obliterated. The body jerked and rolled onto its back, spasmed once and was still. Bolan had won.

But even as the Rifleman died, the RPD opened fire again. This time they had a target. Their rounds poured into the hootch where Bolan hid, whipping through the thatch, creating clouds of dust. He dropped to the floor and rolled onto his shoulder. The warrior didn't return fire because it was no longer necessary. Instead, he crawled to the rear of the hootch and out the door, sprinting across the compound until he reached the berm. He turned once and watched as the thatched roof of the headquarters caved in, a shower of sparks and a rolling flame boiling into the morning sky.

Bolan crawled under the wire and raced across the open field on the east side of the camp. He stopped once, as the machine gun fell silent again, but he didn't wait for the Vietnamese to decide to sweep out of the jungle opposite him. He sprinted across the open ground, bending low, his rifle clutched in his left hand. In a few seconds he made the safety of the trees.

He threw himself onto the ground and used the scope of his rifle to search for the enemy. The camp remained deserted. The fire in the headquarters hootch had burned low but had spread to the nearby buildings. Flames leaped into the air, almost concealed by thick, billowing smoke.

Bolan watched the scene for a couple of minutes, satisfying himself that the Vietnamese weren't giving chase. He got to his feet, picked up the equipment he'd left behind and moved deeper into the jungle. Ryan was lying on the ground, on his back, staring into the trees. Fresh blood stained the bandages at his shoulder and hip. The skin that was visible looked waxy, and his breathing was rapid and shallow.

As Bolan approached, Ryan tried to sit up but couldn't. "I've had it."

Bolan crouched near the badly injured agent, slung his rifle and lifted the man's head, offering him a drink from his canteen. "Drink this."

Ryan turned his head away. "Don't waste your water on the dead."

"Take a drink. I need your help one last time."

"There isn't much I can do." His face was covered with sweat, and the effort to talk was draining what little strength he had left.

"Just listen to me. We've got to go over the escape plan. I'll tell you my plan, and you suggest that I go toward Phan Thiet. Your escape was arranged through there. It's to misdirect any pursuit."

Ryan closed his eyes. "I'll try." Pain racked him, distorting his features. The blank look on his face said that he didn't understand but was too weak to question Bolan about it. He would just trust the Executioner.

Bolan slipped his canteen into its holder. "I'll help you up when you're ready."

"Okay."

Bolan lifted him to his feet. Ryan leaned against him and groaned.

"Only a short distance. Then you can rest."

They reached Rachel Jamison, and it looked as if she hadn't moved during the night. Bolan helped Ryan to sit down and went to remove the gag from her mouth. "You want a drink?"

"Just untie me," she demanded.

If Bolan needed any more proof that she worked for the enemy, he had it in that statement. An innocent woman would have been angry at her treatment. She would have shouted at him, told him what a bastard he was. But she accepted the unfair treatment with an attitude that suggested she wasn't as innocent as she'd like him to believe.

Using his knife, Bolan sliced through the ropes that held her ankles together. When they were free, she straightened her legs slowly, groaning at the effort. Her knees had stiffened, having been held in one position for so long. Bolan moved around and freed her wrists. They were chafed and bruised, showing that she had struggled long and hard to free herself. "I'm sorry about this, but I couldn't take a chance on you."

She didn't move right away. She sat with her back to the tree, breathing easier now.

Ryan rolled over. "Phan Thiet. You can get out through there. Junk at three in the morning. On the beach. Go." There was a gurgling in his throat, and his eyes rolled up in his head.

Bolan leaped to him and lifted his head. Ryan's eyes were dilated, and there was no evidence that he was breathing. Thomas Ryan had died, a brave man who had used the last of his strength to help Bolan make good his escape, had used the last of his strength to provide the information for the diversion.

"He's dead." Bolan glanced up. Jamison had gotten to her feet and was swaying slightly, but she was also trying to get away. She was slipping deeper into the trees as if afraid of Bolan, wanting to put distance between them. It couldn't have worked better for him. He'd wondered how he could get rid of her in such a way that it wouldn't look as if he'd figured out she was an enemy agent. Now she had taken that problem out of his hands with her belated escape attempt.

The instant that she was concealed by the vegetation, Bolan was on his feet, moving toward the jeep. He glanced behind him once, but Jamison was apparently heading for the Vietnamese camp, hoping to get help there and to tell them that Bolan would be escaping through Phan Thiet.

He tossed his gear into the rear of the jeep and pulled out the map. He could move toward the coast, using the back roads and tree lines as cover. When he neared Saigon he'd have to stop and wait for dark. Then it would be a simple thing to get around that city, heading for Vung Tau. The Vietnamese, if Jamison found anyone who could pass the information, would look for him in Phan Thiet. He'd have to hope they didn't figure too soon that she'd been tricked, and that Ryan's escape route was still open.

Bolan climbed behind the wheel and started the engine. It sounded unnaturally loud in the silence of the late morning, but no one opened fire on him and no one rushed from the trees with their weapons drawn. Bolan slipped the vehicle into gear, backed up and turned. He'd need only a little luck to get out now thanks to Ryan. He'd been a brave man, and Bolan felt bad about leaving his body, but there was nothing he could do about it.

He shifted into first and began the short journey to Vung Tau.

EPILOGUE

Bolan sat in the conference room at Fort Bragg, waiting to be debriefed by Colonel Moore. He still found it difficult to believe that so much had been crammed into so short a time. It had been a wild time for him, but then so many old scores had been settled.

Moore entered the room and sat without preamble. He held a file folder with big red Secret stamps on it. "I've read this report. Anything you want to add?"

"I think it's all outlined there."

"Then I have a couple of questions. Before I act on some of this information, I have to make sure we're not jumping to some conclusions here."

"Fire away." Bolan leaned over and lifted the pitcher in the center of the table. He poured himself a glass of water and sat back.

"Ryan was positive about the source of the leak?"

"He seemed to be. Only one man in Bangkok knew who he was and what he was doing. If you check it out, I think you'll learn a few things that will lead right to him."

Moore nodded. "He has a girlfriend named Rachel Jamison...."

Bolan grinned. "That makes it clear, if someone had told McDonald I was there."

"I'm afraid I alerted him as a courtesy to his Agency. We don't think he's a double, just that he's incredibly stupid."

"Which is enough to get people killed."

"Yes. McDonald has been recalled."

Bolan nodded. "There's one thing I didn't put into that report. As you know, the men held there were French, held since the end of their war in Southeast Asia. If the Vietnamese would hold French soldiers for thirty-five years, there's no reason not to believe that they're also holding Americans."

"A logical assumption, but one that we can't make lightly," Moore replied.

"Why not?"

"Think about it. Our President declared that we had achieved peace with honor. Then the North Vietnamese renege on the deal by holding a couple hundred of our men. Everyone pretends that they were all released, but rumors persist. What can you do? We don't want to start another war."

Bolan felt his blood boil. Men had been asked to sacrifice everything in a halfhearted effort to keep the Communists from winning in South Vietnam, and then those captured had been sold down the river. The government didn't think enough of the men to make sure everyone had been returned. Turn your face and pretend not to see. Ignore the fact you owed those men something. Owed them enough to make sure the enemy was dealing fairly.

People could talk about black days in American history, but if men were still being held while the government worked to cover up the knowledge, then it was one of the blackest days. He'd been sent on a covert mission to learn the truth, and although he'd found no Americans, other than Ryan, he wondered what would have happened if he had. Would the government have ignored his report, buried it in the bureaucracy of Washington? Or would they have acted on it and initiated new rounds of diplomatic negotiations to have our soldiers returned?

Bolan suddenly didn't like the smiling man who sat across the table from him, didn't like the smoothness of his approach or his attitude. "Is that all?"

Moore flipped through the folder. "Yes. That's all. Except that all aspects of this mission are classified and any release of this information to the public will result in legal action."

Bolan stood. "Then I think I'll get out of here before I get sick." He left the surprised Moore sitting there, not understanding Bolan's sudden anger.

The warrior left the building rapidly, but stopped in the hot afternoon sun. He watched the soldiers training on the open field across the street, watched a group of them cleaning the grounds and hoped that his gut feeling was wrong. He prayed that there were no Americans being held hostage in Vietnam. But at that moment he didn't have the answer. His trip into Vietnam certainly hadn't provided any new information. All he could do was hope that all Americans had come home.

DON PENDLETON's
MACK BOLAN ®

More SuperBolan bestseller action! Longer than the monthly series, SuperBolans feature Mack in more intricate, action-packed plots— more of a good thing

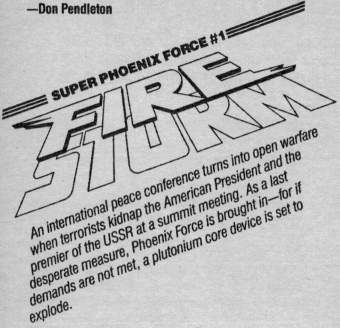

"Gar Wilson is excellent. Raw action attacks
the reader from every page."
—Don Pendleton

SUPER PHOENIX FORCE #1

FIRE STORM

An international peace conference turns into open warfare
when terrorists kidnap the American President and the
premier of the USSR at a summit meeting. As a last
desperate measure, Phoenix Force is brought in—for if
demands are not met, a plutonium core device is set to
explode.

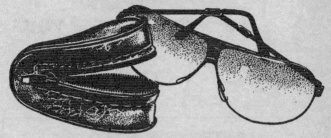

You don't know what NONSTOP HIGH-VOLTAGE ACTION is until you've read your 4 FREE GOLD EAGLE NOVELS